SERIES

...AND FUNNY'
The Times

'WONDERFULLY INVENTIVE'
Daily Express

'AN ENCHANTING STORY'
CBBC Bookclub

'ORIGINAL AND HUGELY ENJOYABLE'
Francesca Simon

'I REALLY LIKE THIS BOOK BECAUSE IT IS FULL
OF FANTASY, MYSTERY AND EXCITEMENT'
Real reader review

'AN EXCITING, PACY READ WITH LOTS OF LUSCIOUS
UNDERWATER DETAIL – MY TWO DAUGHTERS
COULDN'T PUT THIS BOOK DOWN'
Real reader review

Also by Liz Kessler

The Tail of Emily Windsnap
Emily Windsnap and the Monster from the Deep
Emily Windsnap and the Castle in the Mist
Emily Windsnap and the Siren's Secret
Emily Windsnap and the Land of the Midnight Sun
Emily Windsnap and the Ship of Lost Souls
Emily Windsnap and the Falls of Forgotten Island
Emily Windsnap and the Pirate Prince

Has Anyone Seen Jessica Jenkins?
North of Nowhere
A Year Without Autumn

Philippa Fisher's Fairy Godsister
Philippa Fisher and the Dream Maker's Daughter
Philippa Fisher and the Stone Fairy's Promise

For Older Readers

Read Me Like a Book
Haunt Me

eMily WindSNap

AND THE
TIDES OF TIME

Liz KESSLER

Orion

First published in Great Britain in 2020 by
Hodder and Stoughton

1 3 5 7 9 10 8 6 4 2

A CIP catalogue record for this book
is available from the British Library.

ISBN 978 1 5101 0421 1

Typeset by Hewer Text UK Ltd, Edinburgh
Printed and bound in Great Britain by Clays Ltd, Elcograf S.p.A.

The paper and board used in this book are from
well-managed forests and other responsible sources.

Orion Children's Books
An imprint of
Hachette Children's Group
Part of Hodder and Stoughton
Carmelite House
50 Victoria Embankment
London EC4Y 0DZ

An Hachette UK Company
www.hachette.co.uk

www.hachettechildrens.co.uk

This book is dedicated to
Helen Thomas and Kate Fletcher.

I have been privileged to work with some wonderful editors over the years — and you are two of the best. Thank you for always helping me to make Emily Windsnap's adventures as swishy as possible.

'There is a tide in the affairs of men
Which, taken at the flood, leads on to fortune;
Omitted, all the voyage of their life
Is bound in shallows and in miseries.
On such a full sea are we now afloat;
And we must take the current when it serves
Or lose our ventures.'

William Shakespeare, *Julius Caesar*, IV, III

CHAPTER 1

Wakey, wakey!'

Mum's voice called to me from the other side of a dream. 'Rise and shine!' she added, as she tapped on my bedroom door.

'I'm awake,' I mumbled, warm with sleep.

Mum poked her head around the door. 'Come on, up you get.'

I turned over and opened one eye. Mum came in and sat on the end of the bed. 'Back to school!' she said, smiling at me. 'Are you excited?'

'Too tired to be excited,' I said.

And too nervous. I didn't say that, though. It wasn't just the first day of term. It was my first new term after an adventure on a pirate ship that had pretty much changed my life.

Except it turned out that it hadn't *really* changed much at all. I was back in Brightport and everything here seemed about as ordinary as it could get. I'd come home for the last few weeks of term before the holidays, but there had been so much going on in my life and in my head that my feet had barely touched the ground. I'd definitely done that now though, and it felt like I had come back to earth with a bump.

I still hadn't figured out how to get myself to stop thinking about big adventures out at sea and concentrate on sitting at a desk, following school rules.

To be honest I wasn't sure I even *wanted* to figure it out. A big part of me wanted to be out there still, sailing the ocean on a pirate ship. Grammar tests and algebra somehow didn't hold the same appeal.

But here I was and, like it or not, I had to accept the adventures were over and get back to normality.

'I'll get you some breakfast,' Mum said. 'Hurry up, now. You don't want to be late on your first day back.'

I got dressed and joined Mum at the breakfast table. She'd made me poached eggs, sausages, bacon and a crispy hash brown. We only ever had a breakfast like that on special days. Usually I just had a bowl of cornflakes.

Mum saw me looking. 'Back to school treat,' she said with a smile.

I knew why she was going to all this effort. My boyfriend – sorry, ex-boyfriend – Aaron, had gone away to live somewhere else. Meanwhile one of my best friends, Mandy, had barely spoken to me since we'd been home. I'd seen her a couple of times but it felt like we didn't have much to say to each other any more.

Mandy and I used to be sworn enemies. When I first discovered that I became a mermaid whenever I went in water, she used to call me names like 'freak' and 'fish girl'. It was horrible. We made up last year, though, and ever since then she's been one of my best friends.

But then I went off having wild adventures and I wasn't sure how to pick up the pieces of our friendship again. I'd wanted to tell her all about the amazing time I'd had at Forgotten Island and on the pirate ship, but whenever I tried it seemed that she wasn't interested. She'd change the subject or look bored or start talking to someone else.

So I stopped trying. We hadn't seen each other all the way through the Christmas holidays. And now it felt like the old days – the days when I dreaded going to school as I didn't have any real friends.

Which made the prospect of my first day back at school about as enticing as a muddy puddle on a winter's day.

I didn't want Mum to worry about me though, so I forced myself to smile back. 'Thanks, Mum,' I said.

'Come on, love,' Mum said as I sat there looking at my plate of food. 'Eat up. You'll be late.'

'I'm not really hungry,' I confessed. 'Sorry.'

Mum reached over to kiss my cheek. 'OK, chicken,' she said. 'Leave it by the sink and I'll give it to your dad. He never turns down a hearty breakfast.'

She got up from her seat, pulled her dressing gown around her, and went to the fridge. 'At least take some fruit with you,' she said.

'I will,' I promised, as I took my almost full plate to the sink and went to brush my teeth and get ready for school.

Mum came out on to the deck in her dressing gown to see me off.

'Have a good day at school, darling,' she said, giving me a quick kiss before I hopped off *Fortuna* and on to the jetty.

Fortuna is our boat. It's where we live. It sits on the seabed, half sunken, so the lower deck is underwater and the top half is dry. Mum lives upstairs as she's human. Dad lives in the watery part below as he's a merman. I'm a semi-mer. That means I'm a regular girl on land but I become a mermaid when I go in water. I mainly live upstairs with Mum but can hang out in the watery deck too when I transform into a mermaid.

'Thanks Mum,' I said. 'Have a good day too.'

Just then, Dad swam around the back of the boat. 'Hey, little 'un. Today's the day,' he said as he wiped a strand of hair off his face. 'It'll be wonderful, I'm sure.'

'Thanks, Dad,' I said.

I blew them both a kiss, hitched my bag over my shoulder and made my way up the jetty.

I didn't know exactly what was in store for me at Brightport High. But as I walked to school on my own I couldn't help mulling over Dad's words and wondering if I would ever again be likely to describe a school day as anything approaching 'wonderful'.

'Come on now, 8P. Let's settle down, shall we?'

Mrs Porter shuffled papers around on her desk while most of the class carried on chatting, emptying bags, teasing each other and swapping gossip.

The first day back after the winter break was never the quietest day of the year. Most of the class were still buzzing from the holidays.

Even normal Monday mornings were like this. You'd think we didn't spend any time together out of school. Truth was, most of those still talking generally spent their entire weekends, evenings and school holidays either together or constantly messaging each other on their phones. It was hard to know what there was left to talk about.

It was especially hard for me today.

In the old days Aaron would have been sitting on one side of me, nudging me and teasing me and making me laugh. Mandy would have been on my other side, talking about the adventures we'd shared over the weekend and hatching schemes and plans for the week ahead.

Today I sat on my own, an empty seat on either side of me as I unpacked my books and tried to look busy. I did my best not to notice the smiles, laughs and whispered gossip all around me. I tried even harder not to notice that no one was laughing or whispering or gossiping with me.

Not that I could blame them. I'd been absent for weeks last term. I'd missed loads of school – and when I had come back, I'd been so taken up with my adventures that I'd barely given school any of my focus.

As I glanced around now, it hit me that if I had the chance I would trade adventures on pirate ships and beautiful islands to be part of one of the smiling groups around me.

No one was offering the trade, though.

Aaron's empty seat on my right felt like a flashing beacon with a notice over it and an arrow pointing to me.

Watch out! Person with no friends sitting right here! Don't come near!

Then Mandy Rushton came into the room, pulled out the chair on my left, shoved her bag under the table and sat down.

For a split second, my mood lifted. She'd sat next to me! Did that mean we were friends again? Could we get back on track?

It had been so horrible not seeing her in the holidays. Thinking about it, I could understand her side of things. I know it must have been hard for her with me being away. Then I hadn't paid her much attention once I'd come home. But if she'd sat down next to me, maybe that meant she was ready to get back to normal too.

I decided to try saying hello. What harm could one little word do?

'Hey,' I said, nudging her arm. I smiled as she turned to look at me.

Mandy's face might as well have had *Leave me alone, loser!* painted on it in permanent ink. She scowled at me, then very deliberately wiped her arm where I'd nudged her and turned completely away from me.

A moment later she was deep in loud conversation with Julie Crossens and I was left sitting there, feeling like a fool.

My face burned with shame and disappointment – and anger. Why was she treating me like this? I hadn't done anything wrong!

I tried to distract myself by thinking about Aaron instead. Even though we'd broken up we were still best of friends. He'd gone to start a new life at Forgotten Island a few weeks ago, and I still couldn't get used to him not being here.

Thinking about him only made me feel even more alone.

'Come on guys, enough's enough,' Mrs Porter said, just loud enough to be heard over the din. Eventually, everyone hushed.

'Thank you,' she said calmly. 'OK, come on, let's use our registration time to do some catching up. I'm going to call on each of you one by one to tell us your favourite thing from the winter break. And I hope you all had a more interesting time than I did!' Mrs Porter smiled as she glanced around the class.

I instantly looked down at my desk, dreading being picked on first. What was I meant to say?

My favourite bit was swimming in the sea with Shona, the only friend I have left.

Shona's my best friend. My other best friend. Maybe my *only* best friend now. She's a mermaid. Full time, not a semi-mer like me.

I might have been away from school for a while but I hadn't forgotten how it worked. Standing out from the crowd was not the best move. Telling everyone that my only true friend was a mermaid and the only time I felt happy was in the sea was not going to be the best way of fitting back in at Brightport High.

Sitting here in the classroom, the fresh sea air felt like a million miles away, and fitting in with my classmates felt more real and more important than sharing stories of my life on the high seas.

For the first time it hit me that maybe *I* was the one at fault, not Mandy. Had I gone on about my adventures too much at the end of last term? Had I listened to her stories of home? Had I even asked about them? Or had I shown zero interest in her?

Was that why we'd barely even seen each other over the holidays?

Mrs Porter's voice broke into my thoughts. 'Sherry Daniels, do you want to start us off?'

'I went out fishing on my dad's boat,' Sherry said.

'Sounds good,' Mrs Porter said. 'Catch anything interesting?'

Sherry shrugged. 'My dad caught loads. I mainly just helped with the ropes and tried not to be sick.'

Mrs Porter laughed. 'Who's up next?' she asked.

Tammy Bayfield put her hand up. Her mum's the editor of *The Brightport Times*. 'The newspaper closed for Christmas,' she said. 'So I got to hang out with my mum every day.'

'Good for your mum,' Mrs Porter replied. 'We all need a bit of time off over Christmas!'

Aiden Harris thrust his hand in the air. His dad owns the local tip. 'My dad took me for a ride in the tipper truck on Boxing Day,' he said. 'We sat in the truck together on the harbour and looked out to sea. Dad wanted to see a dolphin. He's lived by the sea all his life and never seen one. He says it's his biggest dream. We didn't see any dolphins, but I still had a great day hanging out with my dad.'

'Succinct as always, Aiden,' Mrs Porter said, in that special sarcastic way that teachers must learn at college as they *all* do it.

On and on she went, around the class. Then she came to me.

'I . . . um . . .' I said. My mind had gone blank and my mouth was suddenly dry. I couldn't think of anything to say. I couldn't think of *anything* nice that had happened.

All I could think was that I'd come back from thrilling adventures on the ocean to a town where I was suddenly out of place, where nothing felt right, where no one wanted me. Either *everything* had changed or everything had stayed the same and *I* was the one who'd changed. It was hard to know which way around it was.

Either way, the result was the same: I'd never felt so out on a limb – or struggled so hard to think of something to say.

'Have you got *anything* to share with us, Emily?' Mrs Porter asked.

Everyone was turning to look at me. I wanted to shrivel into a ball and hide under my seat.

I shoved my hands in my pockets so no one would see that they were shaking. My fingers closed around a stone that I'd been carrying with me everywhere. A smooth, oval stone that fitted perfectly in my hand.

Millie had given it to me for Christmas.

Mystic Millie is a part-time fortune teller, part-time hypnotist and full-time best friend of my mum's. She'd bought the stone at a craft fair when she was reading palms on the next stand; it was deep, shiny grey with three bright white lines around its middle. Millie said it's called a wishing stone because it gives its owner three wishes.

She believes in magical things, even though she's an adult, and she knew I'd like it too. It was a beautiful stone and I liked having it near me.

Before I could stop myself I'd pulled the stone out of my pocket and held it out. 'This,' I said. 'It's a magic stone.'

Half the class burst out laughing.

My face burned. 'I mean, obviously, it's not real magic,' I went on quickly. 'It's just, well, it's pretty. I like it.' My voice trailed off. I sounded like an idiot.

Then I remembered something. The stone had come with a poem attached to it. If I shared that, maybe I could rescue the situation and sound a bit more grown up. I pulled out the piece of paper.

'I mainly like it because it came with a poem,' I said. Before Mrs Porter could stop me, I'd unfolded the paper and started reading aloud.

'Make your wish and make it fast.

But don't expect your dreams to last.

Hurry up now, time won't wait.

Slip through worlds and meet your fate.

When you have a magic stone,

Hold it close to take you home.

Life will never be the same

Once you've looked through its dark frame.'

The class was absolutely silent. Were they in awe of a beautiful poem, or did they simply not know how to respond to me making a complete fool of myself?

Finally Mrs Porter cleared her throat. 'That's lovely, Emily,' she said. 'Thank you for sharing something so special with us.'

I could detect sympathy in her voice. The look in her eyes said, *Oh you poor, friendless thing. The best thing in your life is a stone – and a scrap of paper with a poem on it. How sad is that!*

Just in case I needed to feel even worse, Mrs Porter moved on to Mandy next.

Mandy sat up straight in her chair and said, 'My favourite thing in the holidays has been hanging out with my best friend.' Then she glanced quickly at me before moving her chair even further away and adding pointedly, 'Julie. The *best* best friend in the world.'

I felt winded. It was like a punch in my stomach, so hard I nearly doubled over. I shoved the stone and the poem in my bag and looked down at my desk, hiding my face so no one could see how hot it had gone, red with embarrassment and shame.

I was completely adrift. All the fierce, happy independence that I'd found on the pirate ship felt as if it had been emptied out of me.

What was the point of being happy and thinking you were powerful if you had no one to share your happiness and power with?

What was the point in learning about life on the high seas if it meant coming home to a place where no one liked you?

What was the point in telling yourself you didn't care about society's rules and opinions when it turned out that actually you *did* care? And that the more you cared, the more you realised what a self-important idiot you'd been to think you didn't.

Mrs Porter had moved on. She was giving us a few pointers about changes to the timetable and the new teacher who would be taking our PSHE lesson. I barely registered her words.

By the time Mrs Porter looked at her watch and said, 'Well, that's all we have time for today,' and everyone leaped up from their seats to file out of the room, I knew one thing.

I had to find a way to get Mandy on her own, talk to her, see if we could fix things.

I wouldn't survive the term unless I did.

CHAPTER 2

I don't know how I got through the day. I went to the nurse at one point. It was during PSHE. I figured it was a new teacher so they wouldn't know if I was there or not. I told her I had a bad stomach and she let me lie down in the sick room for an hour.

Only, it turned out even *that* was a bad move. Two minutes after I got there a Year Seven kid came in and spent the whole hour coughing, sneezing and sniffing. If I hadn't really been ill when I went in there I was pretty sure I'd have picked up some kind of bug by the time I left.

At least it had given me some time to think. Mostly I thought about how much I wanted to fix things with Mandy. So I gritted my teeth and forced my way through the day.

And now it was time to go home – and I was ready to confront this head-on. A group of kids from my class were hanging around at the front gate. Aiden and his mates were there with Julie and Mandy. I took my courage in both hands and walked over to them. No one turned around as I approached, but I tapped Mandy on the shoulder.

'You walking home?' I asked her. I tried to keep my voice casual. Like I wasn't bothered either way. I didn't want to seem desperate.

Mandy turned slowly to face me. She stared at me for a second then turned back to the others.

That was it. She'd blown me off again and was about to make fun of me in front of half the class. Well, I wasn't going to hang around for that.

'Never mind,' I said as I pulled my bag on to my shoulder and started to move away.

But then Mandy said, 'I'll call you later,' to Julie and turned back to me.

I stared at her, my eyes wide and jaw open.

Mandy shrugged. 'We live in the same direction,' she said.

We walked along in silence for a bit. Now we were together I didn't even know what to talk about.

'Look, I'm sorry I—' I began.

At the same moment, Mandy said, 'What did you want to—'

We stopped walking, stopped talking and stared at each other for a moment. The horrible tension went up another notch.

'You go first,' Mandy said, heading off again.

I spoke quickly as I jogged to keep up with her. 'I just – look, I know that I haven't really been around much lately,' I said. 'And I know I've been doing stuff that, well, that most people don't get to do. It's not like I want you to hang around waiting for me, and not be friends with anyone else . . .' My words trailed away.

'But . . .?' Mandy prompted me.

I sighed. 'But I'd love to pick up the pieces again.'

Mandy's face softened. She smiled. 'Yeah, me too,' she said.

'I mean, I know how hard it must have been for you,' I went on. 'I get that you were jealous of me having so much—'

Mandy had stopped walking. 'I was *what*?' she asked.

I stopped too and looked at her. 'I . . . you . . .' I began. 'I mean, it's understandable. You were stuck here at school and I was out there having all these adventures. Anyone would have felt the same way.'

Mandy shook her head as she laughed bitterly. 'You think I was *jealous* of you?' she burst out.

'I . . . Well, yes. That *was* what I'd thought,' I said uneasily.

'You really have a nerve,' Mandy said. 'You just don't get it, do you?'

'Don't get what?' I asked, feeling my throat constrict. Things had only just started going well. What had I said wrong?

'So you have a bit of a holiday on a tropical island? Big wow. And then five minutes later you make some new friends and go adventuring on some big pirate ship – and you think the problem is that I'm *jealous*?' Mandy shook her head. 'Honestly, I was giving you a chance to apologise to me. I shouldn't have bothered.'

I could feel my face heating up. 'Me apologise to *you*?' I asked. 'What for? What am I supposed to have done?'

'What, you mean other than look down your nose at the rest of us since you got home? Or do you mean other than going on and on endlessly about your *amazing* new friends and how *no one* has ever understood you so well?' Mandy's voice was thick with anger as she stared at me.

I stared back. I didn't have any words. I mean, yeah, I might have been a *bit* like that. But what was I meant to do? Come back home and never mention it?

'If you were a real friend you'd have wanted to hear about it,' I said before I could stop myself.

'Don't talk to me about *real* friends,' Mandy said. 'I'm not the one who drops everyone and everything the minute there's something more interesting to do. The minute there's somewhere more exciting to be than Brightport. I'm not the one who's been acting like the world's ended just because I've had to come home to boring old Brightport.'

'I didn't drop you and I never said Brightport was boring,' I countered.

'You don't *need* to say it,' Mandy replied. 'It's written all over you. Ever since you got home you've been acting like you're just not interested in anyone around here.'

'I've been upset,' I protested. 'Aaron's gone.'

Mandy feigned a yawn. 'That again,' she said. 'Yeah, Aaron's gone – but *I* haven't. I'm still here. Hello! Oh sorry, I forgot. I'm not good enough for you.'

'That's not fair,' I said weakly. But the trouble was, I could see her point of view. I'd been so wrapped up in the things I'd been doing over the last few months that since I'd got home Brightport *did* feel dull in comparison. It was hard to adjust to it again. And yeah, I probably had gone on about Aaron quite a lot – the few times Mandy and I had got together at all.

'I'm sorry,' I said in a quiet voice.

We walked on in silence for a minute. Then Mandy said, 'Look, it's not just you.'

'What's not just me?'

She hitched her bag higher on her shoulder as she walked. 'Me being this fed up,' she said. 'There's stuff going on at home.'

'What's going on at home?'

She squinted at me. 'Come on. You don't really want to know.'

'I do! Of course I do. That's what I'm trying to tell you!'

'My family's problems don't exactly live up to the kind of things you've been dealing with lately.'

I stopped walking and touched her arm. Mandy stopped too. I looked her in the eyes. 'Look, can we start this again? You are one of my best friends. At least you *were* – and I want you to be again. And if you've got problems then of course I care about them. OK?'

Mandy looked at me for a moment. Then she shrugged. 'OK. I'm sorry too. I suppose I was out of order.' She pulled a face. 'And you're right, maybe I was a bit jealous.'

I grinned at her. 'Jealous of nearly being caught up in a major earthquake or jealous of being held prisoner on a pirate ship?'

Mandy allowed herself a tiny smile back at me as she started walking again. 'Well I *was* jealous of the adventures,' she said. 'But now you put it like that ...'

It felt good to laugh with her.

'I mean it,' I said. 'I'm really sorry. It's more my fault than yours. I came back full of ideas and I probably seemed like I was full of myself. Can we start over?'

Mandy nodded. 'I'd like to.'

'So tell me,' I insisted. 'Please. What's been going on? What's happening with your family?'

Mandy looked down at the pavement as we walked. 'Just, things are difficult at home,' she began. 'You know how Mum and Dad opened the new theme park last year?'

'Yes, of course.'

'Well, they put *all* their money into it. They thought we'd be rolling in it from the takings, but it wasn't as busy as they'd hoped last year, and the upkeep is going bonkers. Two of the rides are already looking well dodgy, another one needs fixing and we've barely got enough spare cash to cover the paint. Mum's constantly sitting at home with a calculator trying to work out where the money for our next meal is going to come from. Dad is busy pretending it's not happening and spending most nights down the pub. When he's at home all they do is argue.' She let out a breath. 'It's awful,' she admitted.

I wanted to give her a hug but it still felt too soon. We'd only just made up and I didn't want to do the wrong thing. 'Oh, Mandy, that sounds horrible,' I said instead.

'Yup,' she agreed.

I looked down at the ground as we walked. An empty water bottle was lying on the ground ahead of us. I was about to reach down to pick it up when Mandy kicked it over the side of the pier into the sea. I nearly said something about her doing that, but I stopped myself. I didn't want to set her off. I guessed she kicked it out of frustration and I wasn't surprised.

We'd reached the jetty where I lived.

'Anyway, it's not a big deal, I'm sure we'll figure it out,' Mandy said as we paused at the jetty.

'I want to help you,' I said.

Mandy snorted. 'I don't think anyone can help us,' she said.

'Well, I'm here,' I said. 'Anytime you need to talk. I'm your friend. Remember that!'

Mandy pulled a face. 'Yeah OK,' she said. 'Let's see how it goes, hey? I'll see you tomorrow.'

I watched her slope up towards the end of the pier. I hated seeing her so miserable – but at least we'd had a conversation. Maybe there was hope for our friendship yet.

I turned on to our jetty and made my way down to our boat, *Fortuna*.

'Nice day, chicken?' Mum called as I climbed through the hatch into the saloon. That's what you call the living room on a boat.

'Yeah, it was OK,' I replied.

'Only OK? First day back after the holidays? I thought you'd be buzzing!' Mum got up from the sofa to put the kettle on in the galley. That's the boat name for a kitchen. 'Want to talk about it?'

'I . . .'

Did I want to talk about it? Did I want Mum to know how miserable and lost I felt? How deflated and lonely? How much of a bump back to earth school had been?

No. Mum had enough to deal with settling back into Brightport life herself. She didn't need me unloading my problems on to her as well.

I forced a bright smile on to my face. The effort made my cheeks hurt. 'No, it was great, honestly,' I said. 'Just tired.' I grabbed a glass and opened the fridge. 'I'm going to get some juice and get on with my homework if that's OK?'

Mum ruffled my hair. ''Course it's OK, love. I've got my book group in a bit. Millie's coming round to hang out with you.'

Even though I'm thirteen and old enough not to need a babysitter, Millie still comes around to look after me. Mum's started calling it 'hanging out' instead of babysitting, but it amounts to the same thing. I don't mind though. I like Millie. She mostly just sits on the sofa and watches the soaps so it doesn't make much difference either way.

'Just nipping to the shops first,' Mum went on. 'We've run out of teabags. You know what Millie's

23

like if she can't make an Earl Grey while she's here.'

'OK, Mum. See you in a bit.'

I took my drink into my bedroom and opened my bag. As I pulled my books out something fell out with them.

The stone.

I picked it up and rolled it around in my hands. The smoothness of it felt comforting. And warm. In fact it was *really* warm. Almost hot.

Strange.

I stopped rolling it around in my hands and stared at it. It looked different. The three white lines around the middle were so bright it was as if there was a light on inside the stone. It was magical.

Magical.

Could it really be a magical stone? Not just a silly story that only people like Millie believed? What if it really *could* grant me three wishes?

I almost laughed at myself. That was how sad my life had become. I was seriously contemplating wishing on a rock!

Still. It couldn't hurt, could it? I was on my own in my bedroom. It wasn't as if anyone could watch me or laugh at me.

And if ever there was a time that I could do with three wishes, it was now.

I had nothing to lose.

I closed both of my hands around the stone and

shut my eyes. Then in a soft voice I said, 'I wish there was a way of making Mandy want to be my best friend again.'

As I whispered to the stone it burned and hummed in my hands.

I hear you, it seemed to say. *I will do my best.*

RAP RAP RAP!

The sound brought me out of the moment so sharply it made me jump. Someone was at the door.

Only one person knocked on our door like that. Mr Beeston. I assumed Mum would get the door so I ignored it. I put the stone in my pocket and carried on sorting my school bag.

RAPPITY RAP RAP!

Oh, yes. Mum was out.

I put my books on my bed and went to get the door.

'Ah. Emily,' Mr Beeston said, narrowing his eyes as he studied me.

Mr Beeston is one of Mum and Dad's friends. He actually spent the first twelve years of my life spying on me and Mum and reporting back to Neptune, but that's all in the past. We forgave him once Dad was released from prison and allowed to live with us.

Dad's not a criminal – not a real one. All he did wrong was marry my mum. In the old days, merpeople and humans weren't allowed to marry. But we won Neptune round and he relaxed his laws last year.

25

We were all friends now. But Mr Beeston still gave me the creeps sometimes.

'Mum in?' he asked, stretching his neck to look inside the boat.

'She's gone to the shops,' I said. 'She should be back soon. Do you want to come in and wait?'

Mr Beeston shook his head. 'Far too busy,' he said. I was quite relieved. I really didn't want to sit making small talk with him while we waited for Mum.

Mr Beeston fumbled in his jacket pocket. 'Just give her this, will you?' he said, and handed me a scrunched up leaflet.

I unfolded the leaflet and read the heading that was written in bold type:

Does Your Business Need the MIDAS Touch? We turn everything we touch to GOLD.

'What is it?' I asked.

'It's all in the text,' Mr Beeston replied, pointing at the leaflet. 'There's a chap in town this week from an investment company called Midas. A Mr Whittaker. He's holding a meeting at the town hall on Friday. I was going to see if your mother wanted to come along. Midas are looking to invest in our town.'

'Really? Why?'

Mr Beeston wiped a non-existent speck of dust from his jacket lapel. 'Well, you know I'm not one to try to take the credit,' he began.

I burst out laughing and quickly turned it into a cough. 'No. Not at all,' I said, hoping he didn't notice the heavy sarcasm.

He clearly didn't, as he went straight on. 'But I happened to be in a very important meeting with Mr Whittaker recently and, I have to say, I think I might have influenced him to visit us.'

'Oh. Right,' I said. 'Gosh. Sometimes I forget how important you are.'

Mr Beeston still hadn't noticed the sarcasm. 'Yes, we had a good chat,' he went on. 'I'm fairly confident that I nearly clinched a deal. I would imagine that Friday is merely a formality.'

'What deal?' I asked.

'They are looking to build a hotel and I'm fairly certain that I persuaded him to choose Brightport. I think our little town could do with a bit of a boost, don't you?'

'Well, yes, actually, I do,' I said.

'He wants to see what else is going on in Brightport, meet some business owners and maybe invest in the town beyond their hotel plans. Boost the whole place. Of course I'll be there to help make things run smoothly. Tell your mum, won't you?'

I shrugged. 'Sure. But she's got book group tonight,' I said. 'So she might not get back to you till after that.'

Mr Beeston waved a hand. 'Whenever. Anyway, can't hang around. Bye now, Emily.'

And with that, he turned to leave and I stood in the doorway watching him walk down the jetty.

My mind was ticking over. My heart ticked with it. I reached for the stone in my pocket. It was still warm. Touching it sent a vibration along my arm.

The stone.

I'd made a wish. And two seconds later, Mr Beeston had brought this leaflet round.

A big company wanting to invest in Brightport. Maybe they would invest in the theme park. This Midas company might be able to rescue Mandy's parents — and I might be able to rescue our friendship.

I pulled the stone out of my pocket. 'Did you make this happen?' I whispered.

The stone buzzed gently in reply.

Suddenly, I didn't care about my homework. Only one thing mattered.

I scribbled a note for Mum and propped it up on the table in the saloon. Then I folded the leaflet, put it in my pocket and ran all the way to Mandy's.

CHAPTER 3

'Oh. Hi.'

Mandy stood in her doorway, scowling at me.

I pulled the leaflet from my pocket and held it out to her. 'Tell your parents about this,' I said. 'There's a man coming on Friday. He wants to invest in Brightport. He's from a big hotel chain that's got loads of money. And they want to spend it on people like your family!'

Mandy took the leaflet from me. 'What? Why does he want to do that?'

'Read it. It's all in there.'

She studied the leaflet, scanning over the text. When she looked back up, there was something different about her. She wasn't squinting and scowling at me any more. She was doing something I hadn't seen her do since I'd come back to Brightport.

She was smiling. At me.

'Em, this is amazing,' she said – in a friendly voice I hadn't heard for a long time. 'I can't believe you thought of us.'

'Of *course* I did,' I said. 'I keep trying to tell you – you're one of my best friends and I want to get our friendship back on track.'

Mandy flung her arms around me. 'So do I,' she said, hugging me hard. 'I really do. I hated us being so weird and horrible with each other.'

'Me too,' I agreed.

Mandy pulled away. 'I'm sorry, Emily. *Really* sorry. I think I let my jealousy get the better of me. It just seemed like you were off having these amazing adventures while I was here with my world falling apart around me.'

I bit my lip. 'I was,' I agreed. 'I really was having amazing adventures – but I came back with my head so full of them that I didn't leave room for your feelings. I'm sorry.'

Mandy grimaced. 'Thank you. But hey, it's not your fault everything's going wrong for my family.'

I pointed to the leaflet. 'Maybe it'll start going right again soon,' I said.

'I'm going to tell my parents now. Fingers crossed these Midas people will choose us as one of the businesses to invest in.'

'I'm sure they will,' I said. 'If they plan to open a hotel, I bet they'd want their guests to have a fantastic theme park on their doorstep!'

Mandy beamed at me. 'Thank you, Em.'

'No problem,' I said. 'And please, do me a favour.'

'Of course. Anything.'

'Next time I'm being an idiot, just tell me. Talk to me and let's sort it out.'

Mandy laughed. 'Ditto. I reckon I'm way more of an idiot than you are!'

I laughed too. It felt so good.

I pulled her into a hug. 'See you tomorrow,' I said.

'See you. And thanks again.'

As Mandy went inside to tell her parents about the meeting, I set off back down the pier to our boat. My mind was racing all the way home. The stone had done this. It *had* to have done it. I'd wished for a way of fixing my friendship with Mandy and seconds later Mr Beeston had turned up at our door and thrust a leaflet into my hand which had turned everything around.

Or was it just a coincidence?

The thoughts whizzed round and round as I walked. I wasn't even concentrating on where I was going.

Till I realised I wasn't walking towards our jetty. My brain was telling me to go home but my feet were doing something different.

My feet were walking in the opposite direction towards the end of the pier. All that weird stuff with Mandy had made me want to go and see Shona. I needed a bit of normal hanging-out-with-a-best-friend kind of time.

I checked my watch. I'd only been out for twenty minutes. Mum would probably still be at the shops. And then she'd be so busy running around getting ready for book group she probably wouldn't even notice I wasn't there. And I'd left a note. It was fine.

I stood at the end of the pier for a minute. I glanced around out of habit. There was no one about. Not that it would have mattered too much. Most people in Brightport knew about mermaids by now.

I took off my shoes, climbed down the rope at the end of the pier and jumped.

The cold of the sea took my breath away. For a few seconds, I could barely breathe. Diving into the sea in January is not most people's idea of a good time. Luckily, mermaids adapt quickly, and soon a familiar feeling began to spread through my body, warming me inside and out. My legs stuck together, my toes disappeared, my tail formed.

I was a mermaid once again, and my world felt happy and right.

I spun around and dived lower, flicking my tail and stretching my arms out as I swam.

Rounding the headland, I swam further down, skimming across the seabed. Tiny fish darted away as I swam across their path. Sand clouds billowed beside me. Crabs scuttled under their rocks. Long trails of weeds reached up as if to wave as I passed by.

The water warmed as I approached Shiprock – the merfolk town where Shona lived. I never knew if it really changed temperature or if I just liked arriving here so much it felt like it did.

I swam around the big rocks at the outer part of the town and across the wide space in the centre. Two grown-up mermaids swam past me, chatting to each other as they passed. One of them had a merbaby in a sling on her back, his little tail sticking out behind him as they swished by. An older merman with a long beard smiled and waved as I swam past him. I smiled and waved back.

Coming to Shiprock felt like coming home. My second home.

I reached the opening that led to the caves on the west side of Shiprock where Shona lived. As I reached her place Shona's mum was swimming out of the entrance. She smiled at me. Her smile was so like Shona's. Everything about her was in fact. She was like a grown-up version of Shona. Same long blonde hair, same sparkly eyes. Even her tail was the same beautiful shimmery green and sparkled as brightly as Shona's did.

'Hi Emily, I'm just going out,' she said. 'Shona's inside. Go on in. She'd love to see you.'

'Thanks, Mrs Silkfin,' I replied, and swam inside.

I'd barely got through the entrance when Shona swam out to meet me.

'Emily!' she cried, grabbing my hand. 'I didn't think I'd be seeing you till the weekend!'

'It's only a quick visit,' I said. 'I just wanted to say hi. See how your first day back at school went.'

Shona goes to Shiprock School. 'It was swishy!' she said. *Swishy* is Shona's favourite word. It basically means something is brilliant. Not exactly the word I'd have used to describe *my* first day back.

'Come on, let's go out and I'll tell you all about it. Playground or Rainbow Rocks?'

'Rainbow Rocks,' I replied. It was our special place, and we hadn't been there for a while.

We swam side by side, talking as we glided along. 'So what did you do at school?' I asked quickly. I'd rather hear about Shona's swishy day than think about mine.

'We started a new research project,' Shona said.

'Oooh, fab. What about? Sea monsters? Coral reefs? Ocean creatures?'

34

Shona shook her head. 'Plastic.'

I stopped swimming. 'Plastic? That doesn't sound very exciting.'

'Who said it has to be exciting?' Shona asked, swimming ahead of me. I thought I detected an edge to her voice.

I laughed as I caught her up. 'Well, you know. Just sounds a bit dull, compared to all the exciting things that you *could* be researching.'

We surfaced when we reached our special rocks. I wiped my hair off my face and looked around. The rocks shimmered and glowed against the low, wintery sun. I swam over to the nearest flat rock and half pulled myself out of the water. Shona did the same and we let our tails dangle in the water below us, sparkling and flashing rainbow colours as the shimmering light from the rocks bounced off them.

Shona squeezed water out of her hair. 'Not everything has to be fun and thrilling,' she said without looking at me. 'Sometimes it's about doing things that are important.'

'Hey, I get that,' I said.

'I know *you* do. I just wish more of you did,' Shona replied.

'More of . . . who?' I asked.

Shona looked down at her tail. 'Well, not more of *you*, exactly,' she said.

'Who, then?'

Finally she looked at me. Her cheeks coloured a little as she said, 'Humans, I suppose.'

'Ah. OK, that narrows it down,' I said, laughing nervously to try to lighten the mood.

Shona laughed too. But it sounded forced. 'It's a big issue for us,' she went on. 'It's ruining our lives.'

I thought back to earlier when Mandy had kicked that water bottle off the side of the pier. 'You mean, like, people not picking up their litter?'

'Yeah, for starters,' Shona said.

'It annoys me too,' I said, keen to show her we were on the same side. 'Really, it does.'

'I know,' she said. 'Seriously, I never realised how bad it was. I mean, I've always been aware of the odd bit of rubbish in the sea. But it wasn't till Mr Finsplash gave us all these facts and figures that I realised how bad the problem was.'

'What d'you mean?'

Shona's eyes grew big and round like they always do when she's fired up by something. 'Did you know that every single minute, an entire garbage truck full of rubbish is dumped in the ocean?'

'Whoah. No, I did not know that.'

'Hard to believe, isn't it. And guess what else?'

'What?'

'They reckon that in twenty years' time, there'll be more plastic than fish in the sea!'

I laughed. 'That's got to be an exaggeration, surely?'

Shona shrugged. 'Maybe. I don't know.'

I didn't know what to say. 'Gosh,' I settled for in the end.

Shona glanced in the sea. Then she spotted what she was looking for and swam over to it. I swam around the rock with her.

'Look,' she said, this time holding up a tin can. 'Stuff like this drifts into Shiprock all the time.'

'Not *all* humans throw rubbish in the sea,' I mumbled, thinking about the way Mandy had kicked that bottle over the edge of the pier yesterday without even thinking about it. I couldn't help being a bit defensive.

'I know they don't, silly,' Shona countered. 'I know *you* care about it too. I just wish everyone else could see what we see. I wish it was Brightport High setting up a project to investigate this, not just us in Shiprock!'

'I'm sorry,' I said, feeling useless.

Shona nudged me. 'Hey, it's not your fault. I'm sure people will sort things out soon. They won't leave the oceans to suffer like this for ever!'

'No, they won't,' I said. 'I'm *sure* they won't. So what do you have to do for the project?'

'We have to do some research into facts and figures and stuff,' she said. 'And then suggest a way to improve things.'

'Wow. Sounds hard. Good luck. I know you'll make a great job of it,' I said with a smile.

Shona smiled back. 'Thanks.'

It was getting late and Mum would be wondering where I was if she didn't see me before going out to book group. 'Shona, I need to go,' I said, slipping off the rock and back into the water. 'I'll see you later in the week.'

'OK.' Shona plopped into the water beside me and gave me a hug before we went our separate ways. 'See you soon.'

As I swam back towards Brightport, my mind churned uneasily in circles. What if Shona's facts and figures were right? What if we *were* making a mess of the oceans?

What if humans really *didn't* care what they did to the sea?

As the thoughts swirled uncomfortably around in my head I could hear something humming. It sounded like when a mobile phone is on silent but vibrating in a pocket. I stopped swimming and felt inside the pocket of my jacket. My stone was in there. I unbuttoned the pocket and took it out.

Holding it seemed to calm me. I closed my hand around it and continued on.

But as I swam something weird started to happen. The stone changed temperature. When I headed out towards the open sea the stone warmed up and felt comforting and smooth; when I turned towards the shore it felt cold and harsh.

It reminded me of when I was little and played a game with Mum. She'd hide something on the boat. When I got closer to it she'd shout, 'Warmer, warmer!' and when I moved away from it she'd call out, 'Colder, colder!'

I opened my hand and looked at the stone. It buzzed and tingled and heated my hand up so much I couldn't help wanting more.

Mum would be fine if I was a bit late home. She'd be rushing around to get ready for book group, and I'd still be back before she left. I had time to see where the stone was leading me. I'd follow it for ten minutes and then go home.

I turned back to the open sea, and the stone purred like a happy kitten. I laughed with pleasure.

There was no question about it. The stone was leading me somewhere – and I had no choice.

I had to follow.

CHAPTER 4

I let the stone lead me out to sea without thinking or worrying about it too much. I wouldn't go too far out. Plus, I knew the ocean around here so well I'd find my way home easily enough.

To begin with, I flicked my tail and held my arms in front of me, following the direction that the stone seemed to want to go. Gently swishing my tail was enough to propel me along and I swam calmly through the blue water.

Then it started to feel different.

It happened quite gradually. The pace changed. I

found that I was moving along faster than I usually swam. At first I assumed I was in a normal current and I enjoyed the ease of the movement.

Until it sped up more and more.

Was I in a rip tide?

I'd been in those before and I knew that the best thing was to relax, not try to fight it. Then once I was out of the worst of it, I'd move out of the current and swim back to the shore. The force of a rip tide always slowed down at some point.

This wasn't slowing down though. If anything, it was getting faster and stronger by the second.

OK, it was getting scary now. I needed to get out of here.

I tried to swim against the flow but I didn't stand a chance. It gripped me and propelled me forwards. I felt like I was on the world's fastest rollercoaster hurtling blindly towards my doom. Or in a rocket, zooming down to earth.

The tide grew stronger and heavier, soon flowing faster than anything I'd experienced.

I reminded myself of other times I'd been in a current like this. I'd been pulled towards a mysterious castle and that had led me to Aaron. I'd been sucked through the world's biggest waterfall and found Forgotten Island on the other side. I'd survived both of those – so I could survive this.

Trouble was, this one felt like both of those added together and then doubled. It was dragging me so fiercely it pretty much wiped my mind clear of any more thoughts.

In the end I had no choice. I gave in and let the tide take me further and further out to sea.

On and on it pulled me. At one point, I'd thought the current was slowing – but it wasn't. It seemed to stop for a split second and then it changed direction. I wasn't being taken out to sea any more; I was being pulled down towards the seabed.

A shiver of anxiety ran through me. *What if I got lost out here?*

Don't be silly, I argued back against myself. I couldn't get lost. I was a couple of miles off the coast at most. I was just outside Brightport where I'd lived all my life. Shiprock wasn't far away – and I was a mermaid. I'd be fine. I'd find my way back.

Even if I was hurtling towards the seabed in a dark and frothing chute of water, faster than I'd ever gone anywhere in my life.

Even if I could hear a humming sound coming from somewhere ahead of me that sounded like a louder version of the humming from the stone.

Even if the last two lines of the poem that came with the stone were repeating over and over in my mind.

Life will never be the same
Once you've looked through its dark frame.

What did that mean? Did the stone have a dark side? Was this it? I tried to tell myself that whatever its 'dark frame' was, it surely couldn't be worse than sea monsters and earthquakes and storms and Neptune – and I'd dealt with all of those!

The water was thick with dark swirling puffs of bubbles and sand. A rumbling sound echoed through the darkness. Ahead of me a shaft of light flickered and dimmed like a fading bulb.

As I zoomed towards it the shaft of light widened and grew brighter. The stone pulled harder.

And then – the strangest thing of all.

The seabed began to open.

It was as if the stone itself were ripping into it, carving a deep chasm through the seabed – and taking me with it.

My body was moving faster than my thoughts. All I knew was movement, rushing water and fear.

All around me, I could only see dust and bubbles and huge billowing clouds of sand. I had to get out of here – but I couldn't. The stone wouldn't let me. It felt like it was attached to my hand, driving me forward, faster and faster, into the chasm that it was boring through the seabed. I was powerless to do anything but hold on and hope the ride would end soon.

I had no idea how long I'd been in there. I felt as though I had blacked out for a moment. When I came round, everything had changed.

The manic frothing rush had turned into a steady river's flow. I was in a long, deep, narrow gap in the seabed. Now that the water had cleared I could see that light again, shining brightly ahead of me.

I knew instinctively that the stone wouldn't let me go until we had reached the light. And the weird thing was, I *wanted* to reach it. Having come through that torrent and survived, I wanted to confront whatever it was that had dragged me here.

I looked around me as I swam through the channel. The steep banks on either side were levelling out. The water was growing shallower. The tide was dropping; soon it had gone altogether. In fact, it had started to feel like I was swimming *against* the flow. I realised that I was now swimming up a river.

The light ahead of me grew brighter with every stroke. I swam towards it. It felt like my only option and the only way out.

My tail was getting tired. Odd. I could normally swim all day and not worry about it. Not today though. Maybe the shock of everything had wiped me out.

I pushed myself on. I had to work my arms twice as hard as usual. My tail was barely moving. It flickered at the very tip, as if making the tiniest effort to propel me along. Other than that it felt heavy and weak.

What was the matter with me? Was it me, or was it the fact that I was swimming against the flow of the water?

Or was it something else? Had something down there in that chasm broken me?

I swam on up the river, pushing as hard as I could and pushing away my questions just as fiercely. The daylight ahead of me was growing stronger and brighter every second. Surely I was nearly there. Wherever 'there' might be.

I swam up to the surface and looked all around me, searching for something I might recognise.

There was nothing.

The banks on either side of the river were growing less steep with every stroke. Before long, they were barely higher than the water. I could see the tops of the banks. There were houses beyond the banks, set back a little with gardens and paths leading to the river.

Soon, I came to a break in the houses where the bank had almost disappeared completely. A stony shore led from the water's edge. At the back of the shoreline the bank went steeply up towards a set of steps and a bridge. Next to the steps was a wooden bench. I had no idea where I was but there were enough signs of life to make it worth a look at least.

Plus I was exhausted and needed to get out and rest.

I pulled myself out of the water and sat on the shore. As I waited for my tail to disappear and my legs to return, I let myself rest, grateful for the chance to stop doing anything for a bit.

As always, my legs came back exactly how they'd been before I had transformed. I'd been wearing jeans earlier and I still was. They felt tighter. They must have got waterlogged and shrunk a bit or something. I didn't worry about it too much.

I shook the pins and needles out of my legs as they finished forming. As I stood up and climbed up the bank my legs felt wobbly – much more so than usual.

They still felt shaky as I reached the steps. I had to sit down. I flopped down on the bench.

After a few minutes my legs felt like they'd fully formed and I'd caught my breath again.

OK, time to find out what was going on.

I pushed aside the anxious fluttering in my chest as I made my way towards the bridge.

I'd left the bridge behind me and was making my way along a road. As I walked I had the strangest feeling. I felt as though I'd been here before. But at the same time I felt as though I had never been here in my life.

Where on earth was I?

I'd been walking around for a few minutes when I turned a corner and suddenly I knew *exactly* where I was. Ahead of me the road would lead to another road. After that, I'd turn a corner and walk on a bit. Then I'd turn left and if I carried on straight ahead it would take me to somewhere I knew really well.

Brightport Pier.

I was in the back streets of Brightport! The opposite side of town from where I lived and an area that I'd hardly ever been to. No wonder I didn't recognise it. I had never even realised that there was a river in this part of town!

Still, I knew where I was now. I almost laughed with relief. All I had to do was walk a few streets and I'd be home.

I hurried along, smiling to myself. What a story I'd have to tell people when I got home! Mandy would find it hilarious. Mum would—

'Hi, Ms Windsnap.'

The greeting startled me so much I stopped mid-step to see where it had come from.

A girl across the road was waving at me.

Ms Windsnap? Who called me that? And who was she anyway? I didn't recognise her. She looked about my age. Maybe she was in the year below me at school.

I didn't want to be rude so I gave an awkward wave in return. 'Hi,' I called back.

It happened again on the next road.

'Hi there, Ms Windsnap!' a boy called as he cycled past me.

I didn't have time to reply that time, as he'd gone by before I'd got over the shock. Why on earth was everyone calling me 'Ms Windsnap'? And how come they knew me but I didn't recognise them?

What was going on? Had I bumped my head in that chasm? I remembered feeling as though I'd blacked out at one point. Had I been knocked unconscious and lost my memory? It was possible. It made more sense than anything else I could come up with. I'd be home soon and Mum would help me figure it out. I picked up my pace.

I hurried to the end of the road.

I darted around the corner.

And then I stopped dead.

I knew this road really well. At the end, the promenade crossed it. The pier was on the other side. This was one of the roads full of rundown shops and scruffy guest houses. One of the streets where a couple of the shops were closed and had boards across them. It was one of the main streets that needed tidying up and sorting out.

Except . . . it wasn't.

48

I looked down the length of the street, my heart pounding hard as I searched for something I might recognise.

The scruffy guest houses had gone. The shops that needed a good clean were nowhere to be seen. There were no boards across closed doors.

Instead there was just one building. A very large, gleaming, glitzy hotel, with its name in huge shining letters above it on a glass sign that spread half the length of the street.

THE BRIGHTPORT MIDAS.

CHAPTER 5

I stopped dead in my tracks. My jaw fell open as I felt the blood drain from my face.

The . . .?

The Brightport Midas?

What *was* this?

I looked around, half expecting someone to jump out of the bushes with a TV crew and shout: 'Got you!'

I mean, it *had* to be a joke. A prank. A . . .

But it couldn't be. You don't demolish an entire street and put up a hotel in a matter of hours, joke or not. It just wasn't possible.

And yet here it was, right in front of my eyes.

I carried on down the road, staring and staring as I walked. The hotel filled the entire length of one side of the street. A massive circular driveway led to an ornate foyer with two men dressed in long grey suits and top hats. Beyond the foyer, I could see a paved garden filled with exotic plants.

The hotel stretched on and on. I came to a row of tall windows and stood on tiptoes to see what was inside.

A swimming pool! Two jacuzzis at one end, a big curly slide at the other, sun loungers all around.

I turned away, shaking my head. What was going on? What *was* this place? Brightport had *never* had a hotel like this.

I glanced across the road. There used to be a few shops and a park on that side. The park was still there. Well, *a* park was there. It was nothing like the park I knew. The one I knew about had a few swings, a squeaky roundabout and an old slide. That was about it. To be honest, I never went there much. It was used more by teenagers to whizz about on their skateboards and spray-paint the walls. The lawn was worn and the pavements were cracked. Plus, half the swings were broken and the slide was bent.

Not any more.

The grass was so green it looked like someone had put a super-saturated filter on it. Trees lined a perfectly paved path through the middle of the park. To the left, the play area had a brand-new slide, a brand-new roundabout and swings, and a brand-new, multi-coloured climbing frame that seemed to stretch halfway up to the clouds.

A cold feeling snaked through my body, wiggling like the rope on the climbing frame. A young child was climbing on it. Her mum was standing close by.

As I stared the mum turned in my direction. She smiled and waved. 'Hey Emily,' she called.

Who on earth was she? How did she know my name?

'Hi there,' I called back, raising my hand in a wave that felt as wooden and forced as the smile I plastered on my face.

I had to get away from here. I had to find something familiar.

I turned away from the park and hurried towards the promenade. I had to get to the pier. Had to get somewhere familiar.

Once I got home it would all make sense, I told myself as I walked so fast I was almost running. I'd get back to our boat, tell Mum what I'd seen, and she'd – she'd what? How on earth would she explain any of this to me?

There *was* no explanation. Unless … maybe I was asleep. Yes! That was it. I was dreaming. I'd wake up soon. I just had to jolt myself awake.

I pinched my arm as I sped up even more. *Ow*! It hurt.

I couldn't be asleep, then. Someone once told me that you can't feel pain in a dream.

So it was real.

I'd reached the promenade. I went up to the zebra crossing opposite the pier. The one where you just crossed when you could because the traffic lights were broken.

Except they weren't. They'd been replaced by a gleaming black and white pedestrian crossing with a sparkling machine on each side. I looked for a button, but there wasn't one. There was just a weird blank screen.

I bent down to look at it.

A second later, the screen beeped at me and the green man appeared. I walked across the road to the pier.

Even that was different.

The first thing I noticed was the theme park. The one with the broken rides and the shabby helter-skelter at the end of the pier? It now stretched halfway along the pier. There were rides and stalls and stands advertising hot dogs and doughnuts.

Where had it all come from?

There were people everywhere: on the rides, buying hot dogs, walking around in warm winter coats and hats, all of them smiling and laughing.

The Rushtons didn't usually open their theme park till the spring.

I turned away from the rides and picked up my pace. I wanted to get home so badly it hurt. By the time I'd reached our jetty, I was practically running.

I stopped short when I got there.

No!

NO!

It couldn't be.

It had gone! The jetty I'd lived on my entire life. The wooden jetty with an odd plank missing here and there, and with a few little speedboats and a couple of beaten-up dinghies on it, and our boat, *Fortuna*, moored at the end.

The jetty wasn't there.

In its place was a wrought iron structure with a barred and bolted gate at the end of it. Moored up along the wrought iron pier were about ten brand-new boats. Some cruisers, some yachts − and all extremely fancy. Probably cost a few million each. The one at the end was even fancier and bigger than all the others.

Fortuna was nowhere to be seen.

Everything I knew and loved had gone. My home, my life − all snatched from under my eyes. I was standing here in the place I had lived for my entire life, and I had never felt so lost, confused and alone.

So I did the only thing I could do. I sat on a bench, put my head in my hands and cried.

I had no idea how long I'd been sitting there. A few minutes? An hour? Time had pretty much lost any meaning for me. But I knew I had to pull myself together. I couldn't just sit here and cry all day.

I looked around. Almost everything I could see was unfamiliar, but then my eyes landed on something. The amusement arcade where Mandy lived. Yes, it had all been done up to look sparkly and bright and brand new like everything else. But the door at the end of the building was still there. Mandy's front door.

Maybe she was home.

Maybe she could help me.

Fuelled by the hope of making some kind of sense of this nightmare, I got up from the bench, wiped my eyes and practically ran to Mandy's front door.

'Can I help you?'

A girl I didn't recognise had opened the door and was squinting into the sunlight.

She looked to be a few years older than me. She was wearing a pair of jeans and a yellow hoodie with 'Midas Enterprises' written across it.

'I ... um ...'

'Oh!' The girl looked at me properly. 'It's you. Ms Windsnap, I'm so sorry. Do you want to come in?'

'Er . . .' I said. I wasn't doing very well at forming words. The girl was holding the door open. 'Yeah, sure,' I said eventually. 'Why not?'

I followed her inside. We went through to the Rushtons' living room.

Except it wasn't the Rushtons' living room. It was an office. There were three desks with computers on them, papers piled up everywhere, an armchair in the corner.

'Sorry,' the girl said. 'It's a bit of a mess. D'you want a cup of tea?' she asked.

'I just came to see Mandy,' I replied. 'Is she around?'

The girl screwed up her nose as she thought. 'Mandy?' she asked. 'I don't think we have a Mandy, do we?'

I swallowed. 'Mandy Rushton,' I said. My voice came out in a tiny squeak.

'Oh, of course. Ms Rushton,' she said. She looked at me strangely, as if asking for Mandy in her own home was unusual in some way. 'She'll be at school, won't she?'

'Really? It's nearly evening.'

'Yeah. Try telling her that. She's a workaholic. Honestly, I don't think that place would survive without her — and you of course!'

I couldn't take much more of this. I was starting to feel claustrophobic. The room felt small, as if it were closing in on me by the second. 'Can I use the bathroom?' I asked.

'Sure,' the girl replied. 'You know where it is?'

As long as it was where it had always been, I did. 'I'll find it,' I replied.

I couldn't get out of there fast enough.

I stumbled to the bathroom. Yes, it was in the same place. At least one thing hadn't changed. It had been redecorated, though. It was all black and white tiles and a walk-in shower now. But it was still a bathroom.

The basin was at the far end.

My legs wobbled as I crossed the room. Looking at the floor, I stood in front of the mirror. Everything I knew had changed beyond recognition. What if I had done the same thing? My breath caught in my chest as I hesitated.

Come on. It can't hurt you, I told myself.

I took a deep breath, tilted my head up, and looked in the mirror. And then the breath burst out of me in a horrified gasp.

NO! Please no.

It wasn't possible. It couldn't be.

I closed my eyes and counted to ten. Then I opened them again. It was still there. The face in front of me.

The face that looked about thirty years old!

I moved my mouth, and so did the face in the mirror. I reached out to touch the glass with my hand. The hand in the mirror reached out to touch mine.

It was me. And at the same time, not me at all. I recognised my eyes. Maybe my mouth, the shape of my nose. My hair was roughly the same length, but a bit darker.

I had lines at the edges of my eyes.

Lines!

I leaned forward to look more closely. Tracing a finger over my face, I felt the tiny lines.

Now I thought about it, I looked down at my body. I remembered when I'd transformed earlier I'd thought my jeans had felt a bit tight. I hadn't given it much thought at the time but now it made sense.

I didn't have the body of a thirteen-year-old any more. I was – how old even *was* I?

What was going on?

My mind felt completely empty and jammed full at the same time.

I had to get out of here.

I stumbled to the door and pulled it open. 'Thanks, I'll see you later!' I called from the hallway.

The girl came hurrying out. 'Are you OK, Ms Windsnap?' she asked. 'You look like you've seen a ghost.'

'I'm not very well. I have to go,' I said.

Before she could say another word, I somehow made it to the front door, stumbled out of it and stood on the pier gulping down fresh air as if my life depended on it.

I was standing outside the gates of what used to be Brightport High and now had the appearance of a medium-security prison.

I looked all over the large metal gates, trying to find instructions on how to get them open.

There weren't any.

I peered into a screen by the side of the gate in case that gave me any clues. Two seconds later the screen bounced to life. A photo smiled up at me. I guessed it was me. It looked a bit like the reflection I'd seen in Mandy's bathroom anyway.

A speaker above the screen made a buzzing sound before a chirpy voice crackled through it. 'Welcome, Ms Windsnap. Come right in.' A moment later, the gates opened.

I walked into the school yard. The gates closed behind me.

I crossed the yard. Same thing happened at the main entrance. A locked door, a screen that knew who I was better than I did – and a minute later I was inside the building that despite everything else still looked, smelled and felt like Brightport High. At last, something familiar.

The only problem was the entire school was deserted. Every corridor echoed and squeaked with my footsteps. Every classroom door I opened led to a shiny, clean – and empty – room.

The girl must have been wrong. There was no one here. In fact the more I thought about it, the more ridiculous the idea was. Mandy at school, late on a Monday evening? As if!

That's if it was still a Monday evening. It could be any day or time by now.

I was about to leave when I had a thought.

I could use the school's computers to go online and see if I could find anything that would help me figure out what was going on.

I hurried along the corridors towards the IT room.

It was locked. And this time, there was no facial recognition screen at the top. I guessed the technicians were the only ones allowed in there.

OK, what else?

Wait. The staffroom was along the next corridor. Surely they'd have a computer in there, wouldn't they? I'd never known the door to be locked. Closed, yes, but never locked. If none of the teachers were around, I could sneak in there and see what I could find out.

It was a plan. It was the *only* plan I could come up with.

So I made my way to the staffroom and silently turned the handle. Yes – it was open.

I poked my head around the door. Empty. A table in the middle of the room was scattered with newspapers and books. Mugs were sitting upside down on a drainer by the sink in the corner. The door at the far end of the room was closed. That was the headteacher's office. Luckily, I had never been called in there. Just seeing the door freaked me out, even when it was closed.

Across the other side of the room, a computer was sitting on a small desk. At least, I *guessed* it was a computer. It was pretty much just a massive screen, and I couldn't see a keyboard anywhere. But it was the only thing resembling a computer screen, so I went over to it and sat down.

As I did, a superimposed image of a keyboard lit up on the desk.

Whoah.

The screen came to life with a bright blue box asking for my username and password.

That was the end of that, then. I didn't have either.

Except, two seconds later, an oval shape formed on the screen, turning round and round until – that same photo of me appeared! A moment later, the computer was up and running.

I stared at the empty screen. What exactly was I meant to do? Find Google and type in, *What the heck has happened to my life and to Brightport and how did I suddenly get old?*

Yeah, I wasn't sure that would work.

So, instead, fumbling with my fingers on the weird keyboard thing, I typed:

History of Brightport.

Then I hit return.

In less than a second, a list of links filled the page. I scanned through them. Half of them were advertising books for sale. The rest seemed mostly about medieval times.

Then I saw one that looked encouraging. It was a link to a newspaper article.

The Fall And Rise Of Brightport. How Everything Turned To Gold In A Small Seaside Town.

I clicked on the link.

CHAPTER 6

Some twenty years ago, the seaside town of Brightport was on the verge of collapse. Shops sat empty on the town's front. Many houses were shabby, others were derelict. Even the historic pier was beginning to look like it was nearing the end of its lifespan.

Then Midas Enterprises moved into town and, just like the king they were named after, they turned everything they touched to gold.

Now our pier is visited by thousands of people all through the year. Our beaches are packed full of happy tourists in the summer, and our businesses are booming.

And of course, the flagship Midas Brightport has turned us into a holiday hotspot.

As we celebrate twenty years of 'Midas in Brightport' we at *The Brightport Times* could not be prouder of our town.

To everyone at Midas Enterprises, led by your talented, generous and brilliant Chief Executive Mr Whittaker: THANK YOU! You have given our humble seaside town a new lease of life.

I stared at the words so hard they started to blur. I couldn't make sense of them.

I scrolled down to a photo below the text, scanning the faces to see if there were any that I recognised. I remembered the name Mr Whittaker. That's who Mr Beeston had told me about. The guy who was holding a meeting about investing in Brightport. Was it the same guy? I wouldn't know. I'd never met him.

All I saw on the photo was a bunch of men in suits. I didn't know any of them.

Except ... wait. The one in the middle, shaking hands with another guy and turning to smile at the camera. I knew *him*. Even if he was twenty years older, I'd always recognise those eyes, that crooked smile, the way he buttoned up his jacket.

Mr Beeston!

What was he doing there? And who was he shaking hands with? Was it the Mr Whittaker guy?

I was about to go back to the links to see what else I could find out when I heard a noise behind me.

I looked to see where the noise had come from and saw the headteacher's door was opening. No! I was going to get caught sneaking into the staffroom.

I glanced around to see if there was anywhere I could hide – but I was too late. The door had opened and a woman was walking out of it.

'Emily? What are you doing here?'

I stared at the woman. 'I . . .' I began. 'I . . .'

'Everything OK?' she asked as she crossed the staffroom.

The woman was kind of familiar and kind of not. Almost like someone I knew – but at the same time I knew I'd never met her before. Her voice was familiar too.

How did she know my name?

As she came closer, I realised I *did* recognise her. Kind of.

She pointed back at the office she'd just come out of. 'You look a bit pale. Want to come in for a cuppa? We can talk about Year Nine.' She laughed. 'Your favourite subject!'

'Um . . .' I began. I had no words – for any of this.

The woman reached out to touch my arm. I flinched from her touch.

'Emily, seriously, are you OK?' she asked, frowning with concern.

It was the frown that confirmed it. I knew that expression so well. Even if it was on the face of someone who had changed almost beyond recognition since I last saw her. About an hour ago.

'Mandy?' I whispered.

'Errr, yes!' she replied, with a nervous laugh. 'Come on, let's go into my office and have a cuppa. Nothing a nice cup of tea won't fix, eh?'

She started walking back across the staffroom. I got up and followed her, walking like a robot, trying to get my brain to make sense of any of this.

I couldn't.

Just like me, Mandy looked about twenty years older than she'd looked the last time I saw her.

Was I dreaming? Was all of this a dream?

'Grab a chair,' Mandy said as we went into the office. I stared around me. *What were we doing in here?*

Mandy saw me looking. She pointed at the stack of books and papers on the desk and grimaced. 'Never ends, does it?' she said.

'What doesn't?' I asked.

She pointed at the stack of papers. 'The admin. They don't tell you the job will be ninety-five per cent paperwork before you get it.'

'The job?' I asked. 'Which job?'

She laughed. 'OK, vocation then. Call it what you will. Now. Tea? Or something stronger …?' Mandy's eyes twinkled with a cheeky hint of a smile.

Something stronger? What was she talking about?

Mandy reached up to open a cupboard. It had a bottle of vodka in it. 'I know I shouldn't but – well it's been a tough first day back.'

Tell me about it.

'Want one?' she asked.

'I'm thir—' I began. I was going to say I was thirteen. But as far as Mandy was concerned, I was more like thirty-three. 'I'm thirsty,' I changed it to. 'I could actually do with a glass of squash if you don't mind.'

Mandy gave me a strange look. Then she shrugged and closed the cupboard. 'You're right,' she said. 'We should probably be sensible.'

She brought the drinks over and sat down at the table with me. As I sipped my drink, I tried to figure out what to say. Should I tell her the truth? I mean, if this was Mandy – some weird, futuristic version of her – then she was one of my best friends. She'd understand. Wouldn't she?

I almost laughed out loud. *Understand?* How could she understand something that made absolutely no sense whatsoever? How could I explain something I didn't remotely understand myself?

67

Maybe she could help me figure it out. We were clearly still friends in this weird alternate universe. Could I trust her?

Did I have any other option?

I wound a strand of hair around my finger. Then I said, 'How did we get here, Mandy?'

Mandy laughed. 'Good question. Who'd have thought it, eh? You a teacher at Brightport High.'

I barely heard the end of what she was saying. I was too busy choking so hard I spurted squash all over the table.

Mandy jumped up to get a cloth. 'Emily, are you sure you're OK?' she asked as she wiped the table clean. 'Has something happened to you?'

Oh, you know. Nothing much. Just, I made a wish on a stone and then it dragged me through a chasm in the seabed, up a river and forward two decades, where I am apparently a teacher and you are the HEAD OF BRIGHTPORT HIGH!

I couldn't put this off any longer. 'Mandy, how old are we?' I asked.

Mandy laughed, maybe a little nervously. 'Thirty-three last time I looked.'

'Thirty-three,' I repeated vaguely.

'Em, what's going on here?' Mandy asked. 'You're acting weird. You know you can tell me anything, don't you?'

I bit my lip. 'You're sure about that, are you?' I asked carefully.

'Of course.'

I thought about it for a moment. What did I have to lose? 'OK, then,' I said. 'I'll tell you. But you have to promise me something.'

'What's that?'

'That no matter how far-fetched it sounds – how crazy, how impossible – you will not think I'm cracking up, and you will believe me.'

Mandy frowned. ''Course I'll believe you,' she said. 'Now tell me what's going on.'

So I did. I told her everything.

Mandy sipped at her drink. She'd gone for the 'something stronger' option once I'd finished my story. I'd stuck with my juice.

'You don't remember anything from the last twenty years?' she asked eventually. 'Nothing at all?'

'How can I remember anything?' I asked. 'I haven't been here! As far as I'm concerned, the last twenty years haven't even happened!'

'Em,' she said carefully. 'Do you want me to call the doctor? He's a good friend. I could get you seen pretty quickly, today prob—'

'I don't need to see a doctor!' I snapped.

Mandy pursed her lips together and nodded tightly. I'd seen her mum do that move. Usually when she didn't believe us.

'It's just — it's impossible,' Mandy insisted. 'The only explanation is that something's happened to your memory. And if that's the case, you need to see someone.'

I thought for a moment. Mandy was right. Time travel didn't happen. It wasn't real. It *couldn't* have happened. But then some people might say girls turning into mermaids didn't happen either.

I decided to try a different tack.

'Mandy, we're best friends, right? We still are, aren't we?'

'I hope so. Especially as we've just moved in together.'

'Wait. What? Really?'

'Yes, really. Look, that proves it. Something's happened to your memory. You don't even remember that we live together!'

'I . . .'

'I knew it would happen one day — although to be fair, I thought it would be me before you.'

'What would happen?' I asked.

'One of us would crack under the pressure. Em, you need to go home.'

'Home,' I repeated numbly.

'Yeah, home. Midas Towers. You haven't forgotten where you actually live, have you?'

I forced a laugh that probably sounded like a witch screaming and cackling over a particularly frightening spell.

'Have you forgotten your fob again?' Mandy asked.

I patted my pockets. There was no key in them. 'I guess so,' I replied.

She reached around the back of her chair, feeling in a pocket of the coat slung over it. 'Good job I always carry a spare, hey?' she said.

I took the key from her. It was a small fob that said *Apt 2516*. OK, that was good. All I needed to do was find Midas Towers and get to apartment number 2516 and I might stand a chance of getting through the rest of the day.

Except what was the point of just getting through the day? I'd still have tomorrow to deal with and the day after that. I still had *myself* to deal with.

'Go and snuggle up with Polo,' Mandy said.

'Polo?' I asked.

'The cat.' Mandy screwed her eyes up. 'Em, I don't like this,' she said. 'I really want to call the doctor. I'm worried about you. You really don't seem yourself.'

I couldn't take any more of this.

'Mandy, listen to me,' I said. 'Please, for the sake of our friendship, don't phone the doctor. Just let me figure this out, OK?'

Mandy held my eyes for a minute before letting out a heavy breath. 'OK,' she said eventually.

'Thank you,' I said, reaching out to touch her arm. 'Look, whatever has happened here, I honestly don't think I've lost my memory. I mean, I know it seems like I have – but it seems bigger than that.'

'Bigger?'

I hesitated for a moment. 'Look, do me a favour, play along for a minute, OK?' I asked. 'Let's pretend that I've actually travelled through time.'

Mandy glared at me. 'Pretend you've travelled through time,' she said woodenly.

'Yeah. Hypothetically, OK?'

Mandy shook her head. 'You never stop making me do crazy things, do you?' she said softly. 'But OK, for you I'll do it. Just for fun. Because, you know, you've been under a lot of stress lately and I know that can make you do some strange things.'

'Stress?' I asked.

'Yeah, you know, the stuff with your parents . . .'

'The stuff with my parents?' I asked.

Did I want to know? Could I take another knock right now?

'I'm sorry, I shouldn't have mentioned that. I know we promised not to keep talking about it.'

I swallowed hard. I could feel something inside me tightening into a knot.

'OK, come on. Play pretend,' Mandy said. 'You've travelled through time. When did you travel from?'

I took a breath. 'The last time I saw you I had just handed you that leaflet from Mr Beeston,' I said.

'The one about the Midas meeting. You hugged me. You were grateful. We were friends again.'

'The Midas meeting? Which one? There have been hundreds over the years.'

I swallowed hard. 'The first one,' I said. 'The one when they were looking for businesses to invest in.'

Mandy tilted her head a little as she stared at me. 'Em, you're talking about a meeting from years ago! You mean the one that started everything, when we were, like, twelve years old?'

'Thirteen,' I said.

'Thirteen then. Yes, that was where everything started. It was the one where the Midas team asked everyone for ideas and said that they would invest in the top ones. And they chose the pier and amusements as their flagship investment. That's the meeting you mean, right?'

I shrugged. 'I guess so.'

'OK, so what exactly did you want to say about that meeting?'

'I saw you on the Monday before it happened. The first day back after the winter holidays. I came round and gave you a leaflet. Told you to get your parents to go to the meeting.'

'Yeah,' she said. 'I remember. What about it?'

'The meeting was due to take place on Friday,' I went on. 'In my world, that meeting hasn't even happened yet.'

'In your world? What do you even mean?'
Mandy pulled her chair closer. 'Emily, I'm serious.
Do you need me to call someone? I can get the
doctor to come. He won't tell anyone. It'll just be
between—'

'In my make-believe world – the one you said
you'd go along with,' I said quickly.

Mandy's eyes locked on to mine. I felt as though
she were trying to bore through my head and into
my thoughts.

Finally, she held up her palms in surrender. 'OK,'
she said. 'OK, let's say I believe you. What do you
want to know?'

'I want some answers,' I said. 'How did we end
up here? What the heck has happened to Brightport?
To us? To everything?'

Mandy let out a breath. 'Where do you want me
to start?'

I grimaced. 'At the beginning?'

'OK,' she began. 'It all started at that meeting. My
parents went along, thanks to you, and they talked
to Alan about—'

'Who's Alan?' I interrupted.

Mandy hesitated. 'Alan? You don't even remember
Alan Whittaker?'

'Oh! Yes. Mr Whittaker.'

Mandy laughed. 'Mr Whittaker. Very formal.'

I wanted to remind her I was thirteen, but the
only way to stop her dragging me to the nearest

hospital was to keep up this idea that we were just talking hypothetically.

'Tell me about the meeting,' I said instead.

'So, Alan made everything happen. Or, rather, he got Midas Enterprises to make it all happen. They put *millions* into Brightport. They fixed up the pier, revamped the theme park, did up a load of shops.'

'Knocked down a load of others?'

Mandy squirmed in her seat. 'That's always been the sticking point for some. I mean, they were good to my family. They literally saved us from ruin, so we've never felt that we can campaign against them. But you've never really seen eye to eye with them. And I don't blame you. I know it's not been easy for you, having a foot in both camps.'

'What do you mean?'

Mandy looked even more awkward. She ran a hand through her hair and picked up her drink, hiding her face behind it. 'Look, they've had to make compromises, that's all. And it's been hard. I know you've made tough choices – but you had to, and no one blames you. Well, I don't anyway.'

Mandy put down her drink and went on before I could push her further. I wasn't even sure I wanted to. I was having a hard enough job dealing with what was going on. I wasn't sure I needed to hear about the tough choices I'd had to make to get here.

'In the end, what they've done has been good for all of us. They've saved the town, put us on the map.

Life has never been so good here, Em. I know you don't always see it that way but without them Brightport would have crumbled – and taken my family and half the town down with it.'

'And everyone's fine now,' I said, letting my voice imply that I was asking a question without outright asking it.

'Everyone's great. Most people still work in town. Sure, they might work for Midas now rather than running their own guest houses – but they get paid more for it and don't have the responsibility.'

'And my parents?' I asked, holding my breath while I waited for her to answer.

'Your parents are fine!' Mandy said. 'Well, your mum is. We – obviously – don't see much of your dad nowadays.'

'Why *obviously*?'

Mandy's face shut down like a door closing in front of me. 'Well, you know, things are just ... different. Everything's changed. A long time has passed. But they're good. You know. They're OK.' Before I could ask anything else, Mandy hurriedly went on. 'My mum and dad took early retirement on their investment. They're three months into their around-the-world cruise as we speak!'

I shook my head. It was a lot to take in.

'And me?' I asked finally. 'Am *I* fine?'

Mandy reached out to touch my arm. 'Em, you're *more* than fine,' she said gently. 'You're fantastic!'

'Really?'

'Really! You're one of the most popular teachers in the school. You're—'

'I'm *what*?' I nearly fell off my chair. Being a teacher was one thing – but being popular at Brightport High? That was a step too far!

'You're really popular,' Mandy insisted. 'Everyone loves you because you're fair and kind and you do your best for everyone.' She paused for a second, and then in a voice that was gentler than I'd heard Mandy use for a long time, she added, 'It's what you're like, Emily – and it always has been.'

I could feel the heat rise in my cheeks. 'But have I?' I mumbled.

'Huh? Have you what?'

'Have I done my best – for everyone?'

'Em, you do as much as is humanly possible,' Mandy said.

And that was when I realised there was a big chunk of unspoken stuff going on between us. She hadn't mentioned me being a semi-mer. She hadn't mentioned Shona, and she'd said that she 'obviously' hadn't seen my dad.

Somewhere amongst all these things about myself that I was trying to catch up with, somewhere inside all the facts that didn't add up, the pieces that didn't fit together, the external facts that didn't match the ones inside me – somewhere amongst all of that there were truths that we weren't talking about. I didn't know if I even wanted to ask the questions.

I was even less sure I wanted to hear the answers.

I pushed my chair back and stood up. 'Mandy, I need to go,' I said. 'Thanks for the drink.'

'Wait – that's it?' she asked. 'You land all this on me and then just up and leave?'

I paused. 'I know. Sorry. Look, you're right. I've been really stressed lately. I think my head's just got a bit overloaded. I'm going to do what you said, go home and cuddle the cat.'

'Oh, and maybe feed him too.' Mandy gestured at the paperwork on her desk. 'I'm going to be home late, I expect.'

'Will do.'

Mandy walked me to the door. 'You *sure* you're going to be all right?' she asked. 'Honestly, I can get the doctor round in two min—'

'I'm fine,' I insisted, forcing what I hoped was a reassuring smile on to my face. 'I promise.'

And before she could say anything else, I opened the door, gave her a quick hug and got the heck out of there.

CHAPTER 7

I walked past the apartment building for the third
time. It hadn't been hard to find. For one thing,
there were signs for Midas buildings everywhere.
For another, Midas Towers turned out to be the
tallest building in town.

It had been built at the far end of the promenade.
Like the school and the jetty on the pier, it was
gated and locked.

I couldn't help wondering if anyone trusted
anyone else around here nowadays, the way security
was. I guessed that was what happened: the fancier

your lifestyle got, the more you had to lose, and the more you needed to protect it.

Anyway. I fumbled with the key in my hand, wondering if it would let me into the gated area and if I'd have the confidence to breeze through and act as though I knew what I was doing.

Turned out I didn't need to worry about it.

'Good evening, Ms Windsnap.' A very tall man with a bright gold uniform and an even brighter smile seemed to appear out of nowhere. 'I trust you've had a good day,' he said as he pressed a couple of buttons on a keypad and the gate opened in front of me.

'Um. Yes. Thank you,' I said. 'You?'

The man tipped his hat as I walked into the complex. 'Just grand, Ms Windsnap. Thank you for asking.'

I walked along the immaculate path that cut through two immaculate lawns and made my way to the huge apartment block in front of me.

Did I really live here?

The foyer felt empty and sterile. A table on the right with what looked like artificial flowers in a vase; two lift doors on the left. I pressed a 'call' button and waited.

Within seconds, the lift arrived and its doors opened. Which floor?

I checked my key fob again. Apartment 2516. Then I checked the buttons on the wall. They went up to 30. Were we on the 25th floor?

There was only one way to find out. I pressed the button with '25' on it and let the lift carry me up.

Half a minute later, I was in a corridor that pointed left for apartments 1–15 and right for apartments 16–30. I turned right. At the end of the corridor, there it was. Apartment 2516.

As I swiped the fob, my hands shook so much I nearly dropped it. A soft click, then I pushed against the door and went inside. Into the apartment that thirty-three-year-old me shared with Mandy and a cat called Polo.

I closed the door behind me and looked around. I was in a large room with a soft beige carpet, a big table covered in books, a squashy sofa along one wall and on the other side, the biggest window I'd ever seen.

I crossed the room and looked out of the window. Below me Brightport was spread out like a toy town. Tiny cars and even tinier people bustled about below me. The sea widened out to the horizon, the edges flowing on to the beach in regular white lines, the blue growing deeper the further towards the horizon I looked.

This was really my home? Maybe the future wasn't such a bad place to be after all.

'YEOOOWWWWL!'

I spun around to see a grey velvety-looking cat skip into the room and jump on to the back of the sofa.

'Hey you,' I said, walking over to the sofa and reaching out to scratch the cat behind his ears. 'You must be Polo.'

The cat purred like an engine in reply.

'Are you hungry?' I asked.

Polo purred harder.

I found the kitchen and stood looking around. The kitchen surfaces gleamed at me. The hob sparkled so brightly it shone. It was like a show home.

Again I couldn't help asking myself: did Mandy and I really live here? Not only was it the fanciest place I'd ever set foot in, I couldn't imagine us keeping a place this clean and tidy!

Maybe we had a cleaner.

After opening a few cupboard doors I found a box of cat food and sprinkled some in a dish. Polo scampered into the kitchen, slid by my legs, brushing against me and arching his back, before digging into his tea.

I put the box of food away and watched Polo eat. My breathing started to calm and I went back into the lounge.

OK, maybe I could do this. Live in this nice apartment with Mandy and a very sweet cat, looking out at that view. It wouldn't be so bad if I was stuck here for ever.

Except for one thing. I wouldn't be able to spend my time hiding from the world in here.

I had a job! I was a teacher!

I left the cat and went over to the table. Picking up the books, I tried to piece together what I even taught. Lots of novels and poetry collections. Did I teach English? Could be worse. It could be physics or something. I wouldn't have a clue where to start with that. With English, at least I could fall back on 'write about your holidays' for a few days.

And then what?

No. I couldn't do it. I couldn't live this life – I'd never get away with it. It wouldn't take long for everyone to figure out that I was a fraud, that I knew nothing. Then what? I'd lose my job, maybe my friendship with Mandy, maybe even my home.

The thoughts were making me panic. Before I knew it, I'd created an entire disaster movie out of my life.

I glanced around the room, trying to find something to anchor me to the life I knew, to anything I recognised. There was a chest of drawers along the far wall, with photos mounted in frames. I went over and looked at the photos.

Most of them were of Mandy and me. Smiling and laughing and surrounded by friends in all of them.

Which should have made me feel better. But it didn't. It made me feel worse – because it made me even more aware of what was missing, what was wrong.

Shona. She wasn't there. She wasn't in any of them.

I couldn't imagine a life without Shona. It wasn't possible.

Fancy apartments and cute cats were fine – but they weren't real. They weren't me. The more I thought about it, the more I knew what I had to do.

I had to go and see Shona.

I walked along the sparkling wooden boards of the pier till I reached the very end, around the back of the swanky new theme park.

The steps were still there, stretching into the sea. I glanced down at the water, swirling and flowing below. In the fading light, the darkness seemed to glisten. I watched it for a moment. Then I climbed down the steps, and dropped into the water.

The first splash was cold. It took my breath away. But I always adapted quickly, so I didn't worry too much. It took longer than usual this time and I shivered as I waited for the change to come.

I dipped my head under the surface and started to swim. Any second now, my legs would transform into a tail and I would become a mermaid.

But nothing was happening. Or, *something* was happening, but it was taking longer than usual. My legs were growing stiffer and heavier, but as my tail began to form it felt almost as rigid and solid as my legs.

I twitched the tip of my tail – the only bit that seemed to be working. It flickered just enough to move me slowly along. I tried again. This time, my tail seemed to flex a bit more. It was tiring work – I was having to force my tail to move up and down. Finally, it began to loosen. It was as if it had been tied up in knots that needed to be undone and freed. It felt as if I had forgotten how to use my tail.

Weird. Why would I forget how to use my tail?

Never mind; it was working now, and I was warming up too. I shrugged off my worries and swam deeper. I was a mermaid now, and I was heading for Shiprock. I was going somewhere familiar, somewhere that always made me feel better.

Everything was fine. Better than fine. Everything was great. And in a moment, I'd be with Shona – which would make it even better!

I'd got as far as the end of the bay when I stopped swimming and looked around. I needed a rest.

Either the thirty-three-year-old version of me barely did anything and my body was just super-unfit, or I simply wasn't used to being a mermaid.

That didn't make sense though. Why would I not spend time being a mermaid? I could barely get through a day without transforming into my mermaid self. It was part of what made me feel alive, part of what made me feel ... me. It was unthinkable that I wouldn't do it.

But that wasn't the only thing that had made me stop. It was the sea itself. As soon as I'd passed the edge of Brightport bay, it started to change.

Inside the bay, the water had been sparkling and clear – even in the fading light of the day. As soon as I'd rounded the headland and was in the deeper water out of sight of the town, the sea seemed to grow denser. To begin with, there were just small particles dotted about. I thought they were tiny fish at first. But as I swam on, the particles were larger – and there were more of them.

What were they?

They seemed like tiny stones, or clods of earth or something. I reached out as I swam, and grabbed a handful of them. Flicking my tail to hold my position, I stopped swimming and opened up my hand. The particles crumbled against my palm and my skin felt gritty. It felt like broken-up concrete. But what was it doing in the sea? And where was it all coming from?

I swam on – but it was getting harder. As I swam, the water grew murkier and grittier with every stroke. Soon I could barely see where I was going.

Maybe if I swam further out to sea it would get better.

It didn't. If anything, it was getting even worse. Soon it was so bad, I could barely see at all. The whole ocean seemed to have become dark, grainy and almost impossible to swim through. And where were all the fish? I'd hardly passed a single one.

I was about to turn and head back for Brightport when I spotted something through the murk. A flash of white.

I swam towards it. As I got closer, I saw that it was a stone pillar reaching all the way down as far as I could see. It had either grown out of the seabed itself or had come from the same place as all the smaller pieces of concrete and somehow been planted there.

I swam up to it. It had an arrow carved into it, with three words carved below the arrow.

MERFOLK: THIS WAY

The arrow pointed left and downwards. I did what it said. It was difficult, as I was swimming against the natural current of the water, but I managed.

A few moments later, I came to another pillar. Smaller this time, and lower down. I swam towards it. Again, an arrow, with the same instruction. This time pointing directly ahead, and again, down.

I swam on. Another minute later, I spotted yet another white boulder in the darkness of the sea. Again, I followed the arrow. I carried on like this, following the trail of arrows until, finally, the water began to clear a tiny bit. I stopped swimming, holding on to the boulder while my body rested.

I looked around. Now that the murkiness had subsided a little, I realised my surroundings were starting to look familiar.

Or at least, half familiar.

I swam on towards a huge rock that formed part of an underwater cave. I knew that rock. It marked the start of Shiprock. There was just one thing about it.

Half the cave was missing.

I flicked my tail and approached the cave. Where it used to be a huge, welcoming entrance to a bustling merfolk town, this was now a jagged rock surrounded by boulders and rubble.

What had happened here? Had there been an earthquake or something? And if so, when? How long had it been like this?

My head spun with questions till it felt as messy and clogged up as the sea. There was only one way to answer the questions.

I swam through the half-rubble, half-opening into what I hoped would still be the merfolk town I loved.

CHAPTER 8

*E*verywhere I looked, all I saw was ruins. Where once there had been elegant caves with entrances adorned with beautiful sea plants and coral of every colour, now it was all muddy water, collapsed caves and rubble.

This wasn't the Shiprock I knew so well.

What had happened?

I passed what used to be the centre of the town. Last time I was here, the wide arched entrance to Shiprock School was ahead of me and everything was bustling with life: mermaids swimming by with merbabies on their backs, old mermen talking in huddles outside their caves. Everyone I saw would smile and offer a warm greeting as I swam past them.

Now the centre of the town looked more like the aftermath of a battle scene from a post-apocalyptic movie.

Yes, there were still a few merfolk dotted around. But none of them swam by. None of them smiled or greeted me. They were all huddled into dark corners, some alone, others in pairs. A couple of them looked really young – younger than me, even. Too young to be on their own. But they *were* alone. Skinny, gaunt and dirty-looking.

No one met my eyes as I swam past, but I could feel them watching me cross the space: a stranger in their midst giving them a reason to scowl with suspicion.

Finally I'd swum past them all and I carried on to the stretch of caves where Shona lived.

At least it *used* to be the stretch of caves where Shona lived. It didn't look like somewhere anyone would live now. The seabed was practically invisible. You couldn't see sand at all, only rocks, rubble and dirt. No plant life. Not a single fish swam past me. No colour. Just grey, dull, dirty water.

Surely no one could live here?

But as I arrived at what used to be Shona's cave – now little more than a small, dark hole in a pile of rubble – I saw someone coming out.

It was a tall slender mermaid with long blonde

hair. She had a green tail. Admittedly, not as sparkly and shiny as it used to be. But as she swam away from the hole, I recognised that straight upright style of swimming instantly. It was Shona's mum! Shona *did* still live there!

I swam over towards her. 'Mrs Silkfin!' I called as I swam.

She didn't hear me. I swam harder. 'Mrs Silkfin,' I said again as I caught up with her. I reached out to touch her arm.

She jumped a little, then stopped swimming and looked at me.

That was the first time I saw her face. She looked different. Her hair was a bit scraggy and knotted, when normally it was as perfectly combed as Shona's. Her face looked scarred and grey where normally it was bright and shiny. Still, she looked similar enough that I knew it was her.

'Hi!' I said.

Mrs Silkfin stared at me, her mouth falling open.

'Um. It's . . . Emily,' I said.

She frowned. 'I know who it is,' she said in a voice that sounded distinctly unfriendly. She'd never been unfriendly to me before. In fact, I couldn't remember seeing her frown before. She only ever smiled, and looked serene and happy. Nothing about this was feeling familiar or right.

I pointed back towards the entrance to their cave. 'Is, um, is Shona in?' I asked.

Mrs Silkfin's jaw fell open even wider. 'Are you *kidding* me?' she spat.

'I ... No ...?'

Mrs Silkfin tutted and turned away.

I reached out for her arm. 'Wait,' I said.

She turned back again. Her face looked pinched and tight. 'What is it, Emily?' she asked. 'What do you want?'

'I ... I just came to see Shona,' I said feebly.

Mrs Silkfin held out her arms. 'Well, now you have,' she said, tight-lipped with fury. 'Happy?'

A cold feeling darted through me. What had I thought? That time would have stood still in the ocean, even though it had gone forwards twenty years on land?

The time had passed just the same here. All those years. The merfolk had grown up without me, just like the people of Brightport had done.

'Shona?' I whispered.

'Oh, well done,' she said sarcastically. 'You finally remembered who I am. Not that I would expect you to recognise me, anyway. Not that you ever visit us here in Shiprock any more.' She turned to leave again. 'Now if you'll excuse me, I've got things to—'

'No!' I grabbed her arm.

Shona looked down at my hand, then shook it away. 'Don't you dare take hold of me,' she said, her mouth twisted with disgust. Her tail was flapping in the way it sometimes did when she was anxious.

I glanced at it, and it made me sad. Like the rest of her, it had lost its shine. Shona, who always took such pride in her appearance, whose favourite thing in the world was Beauty and Deportment lessons, was a shadow of her former self.

'What's happened to you?' I croaked. My throat had tightened up with emotion.

Shona stared at me again. Her sad, dull, grey eyes wide. 'What's happened to *me*?' she echoed. 'Are you *seriously* asking me that?'

'Yes, I—' I began. She didn't let me get any further.

'*You* have happened to me,' she snapped, her tail flicking and her voice high pitched with anger. 'You and the rest of your human friends. Your beautiful town, your lovely houses and hotels, all your shiny, sparkly perfect streets, your perfect lives. Yes, you spent a year or two acting as if you cared about us, but in the end you gave up, didn't you? You let them demolish our lives so you could build yours up and forget all about us.'

'Shona, I don't know what you're talking about,' I said. 'I haven't been—'

'Don't insult me by pretending you don't know,' she said. 'It's been years since you came here, Emily. Sure, you went to a few meetings, spoke to a few people. But you didn't try hard enough. And now look! I'm living in squalor and you're a happy popular teacher.' Shona clapped her hands together. 'Well done you,' she said with a horrible, sarcastic smile.

'Shona, will you listen to me?' I pleaded.

She shook her head. 'No Emily, I won't. I'm not one of your *adoring* students. I don't have to listen to *anything* you say.' And with that, she started to swim away.

I swam after her. 'Shona!' I began. She swam faster. I twirled my tail to pick up my pace and keep level with her. 'Just give me two minutes. Let me explain. Please!'

Shona swam on for a bit, then suddenly stopped. Spinning her tail in a fast circle to keep her upright, she nodded briskly. 'Two minutes?' she asked.

'Yes.'

'To explain twenty years?'

'Well, to *begin* to explain.'

'All right,' she agreed. 'I suppose I can spare two minutes.' Folding her arms, she turned her eyes on me like a harsh beam of light. 'You'd better get on with it; your time's already started.'

I wasted the first ten seconds wondering when Shona had turned so cold and brittle, what exactly had made her that way and why our friendship hadn't survived the years.

Then I started talking. 'I'm not who you think I am,' I began. 'I mean – I am. I'm Emily. But not the Emily you're seeing.'

Shona glared at me. 'That's the best you've got?' she asked. 'You're not really *you*? I can't believe this.' She turned away again. 'I haven't got time for—'

'Yes, you have!' I broke in. 'You said you'd give me two minutes. I haven't even used one of them yet.'

Shona flicked her hair. I tried not to wince as I watched her. The gesture was classic Shona but where her hair used to flow and shine, spinning around her in the water like a golden halo, now it hung loose and lank and tangled a little from the movement. Anyway, I had to keep talking.

'You're not going to believe this,' I said, talking as quickly as I could, 'but I have slipped through time. I have gone through some kind of – I don't know – like a portal. This river opened up in the seabed and it's carried me through time.' I jabbed a finger at my chest. 'In here, inside my body, I am thirteen years old,' I whispered. 'I've lost twenty years.'

Shona stared at me. 'I honestly don't know what you think you are—'

'I still have half a minute!'

She clamped her mouth shut and I carried on, talking even faster. 'I have literally no idea what has happened. I don't know why I deserted you, I don't know *when* I deserted you – but I know that I want to make amends. Shona, you are my best friend. You always will be. We've been on so many adventures together, we've been in all sorts of crazy and scary situations together. But believe me, I have *never* been as scared as I am now. I have no idea what has happened, but I swear to you, I have lost

95

twenty years and I do not know where they have gone.'

I stopped speaking. Partly because I reckoned I'd used up my two minutes, but more because it felt like something the size of a giant rock was lodged in my throat and I couldn't get any more words past it.

I felt a tear run out of each eye, slipping down my cheeks and mingling with the taste of the sea water as they hit my lips.

I'd played my hand. I'd given my best friend the best version of events I could. Now all I could do was wait for her response, and hope more than anything in the world that she would believe me.

Shona didn't say anything for ages. She just carried on looking at me. When she spoke, her voice was as heavy as iron.

'I don't know if this is some kind of elaborate hoax to draw me in so you can destroy our lives even more—'

'It's not a hoax,' I broke in. 'Why would I make up something like this? Why would I want to destroy your life?'

'I've asked myself the same thing many times,' Shona said. 'I still don't know the answer. You tell me.'

'I can't,' I said weakly. 'I don't know.'

Shona let out a bitter laugh. 'Typical. You don't know. It's not your fault. Honestly, you're all the same: Brightport High, your corrupt council, greedy Midas – and you. I thought you were better. I thought you were my friend. I never thought you would really let it happen.'

Shona waved a hand to indicate the state of Shiprock, the ruins it had become.

'You're saying *I* did this?'

'OK, whatever. It was Midas, mainly. They killed the place when they moved into Brightport nineteen years ago with their trucks and diggers and armoured vehicles. It looked like an army was coming into town the day they arrived. We watched together from Rainbow Rocks. Don't you remember?'

I held my arms out in a helpless shrug. 'Shona, I don't remember *any* of it, because I wasn't there. I haven't been here. You have to believe me—'

'Save it, Emily,' Shona cut me dead. She paused for ages. Then in a quieter voice she went on. 'I get it. Honestly, I do. I know you tried at first. I know they're bigger than us. I know you had to make some tough calls. Just – well, I suppose I'm disappointed that the calls you made drove us apart.'

My jaw hung open. I literally didn't know what to say.

Shona's lank hair fell into her eyes and she wiped it away. 'They lured you on to their side. All of you.

First, Mandy's family. Then you too. Even before we'd finished school, they had you. Offering bribes to get you to leave your home behind so they could turn the pier into a massive theme park. Then the training after school. The promises, the lies, the money, the yachts.' She shook her head.

'Shona, I don't know what you're—'

'Even then, I thought you'd never desert us,' Shona went on as if I hadn't interrupted. 'I understood it was hard for your mum to turn them down. And I know, I *know* you tried. But then you said yes to their swanky training programme the minute school was finished, and from that point onwards I knew there'd be no turning back. You were one of them. They owned you. They bought you.'

Shona's words weren't making any sense. They were swimming around, getting inside my head but refusing to join together into anything I could understand.

'They made you choose,' Shona went on. 'And yeah, I understand that it wasn't much of a choice by that point. You had to live. But – I just never thought you'd abandon us.'

'I . . . I can't believe I would either,' I said. 'I *wouldn't*.'

Shona shook her head again. 'Whatever. They had you over a barrel, like everyone else in that shiny golden town. You made your decisions and I've had to accept them ever since. And then you became a teacher and I could count on my gills the number of times I've seen you since then.'

'When did I start my teaching job?' I asked.

Shona screwed up her nose as she thought. 'A little over ten years ago now,' she said. 'Just before they started the full-scale building project.' Shona's voice cracked a little as she went on. 'Just before the cliff face fell away, and they brought in the underwater pipework to hold it up – destroying half of Shiprock in the process.'

I could hardly believe what she was saying. 'But – they wanted to do a building job like that last year, do you remember?'

'Last year? More like twenty-one years ago,' Shona said bitterly.

'We got the council to agree not to do it back then,' I whispered. 'We kept Shiprock safe.'

Shona glared at me. 'Yeah,' she said. 'That was before Midas started lining the pockets of the Brightport councillors. One by one, they miraculously changed their tune. Cut forward two decades and here we are: Brightport is thriving while Shiprock is crumbling and dying.'

I didn't know what to say. I could hardly speak anyway, even if I did have words.

I reached out to touch Shona's arm. 'I can't let this happen,' I said in a croak, feeling more useless than ever.

She looked at my hand, but didn't move her arm. 'It already has, Emily,' she said sadly. 'It already has.'

'I just can't bear it,' I said in a whisper. 'Us. Shiprock. Everything.' My throat hurt as I spoke. I wasn't sure how much more of this I could take.

I needed someone to tell me that we could fix it. I needed my mum.

As soon as I thought it, I realised how true it was. I didn't even know where she lived any more, but I had to find her. I just needed someone to hug me and tell me it would all be OK.

'Shona, I have to go,' I said.

'Surprise, surprise,' she said. 'Leaving me again. Just like you always do. Good job I don't expect anything different from you nowadays.'

'Shona, I am not leaving you!' I insisted. 'I'm going to find a way to make things right.'

'OK, good luck with that,' Shona said, flicking her lank hair.

I looked fiercely into her eyes. 'I'm not leaving you like this. I'm not letting the future end up like this,' I said. 'I don't know how. I don't know when but I'm going to fix this.'

Before she had a chance to reply, I turned, flicked my tail and swam back towards Brightport. I would prove to Shona that I was telling the truth. I would find a way to sort out this awful mess, even if it killed me.

I just hoped it wouldn't *actually* come to that.

CHAPTER 9

I pulled myself out of the water and perched on the steps as my tail flickered and twitched. After a few minutes the flickering stopped and in its place a numb feeling spread through my tail. A moment later my tail faded away completely and my legs returned. I rubbed my legs to get rid of the pins and needles that the transformation always gave me. Then I clambered up the steps and back on to the pier.

I didn't have a plan. I walked up the pier without even thinking about it, almost on autopilot. I barely even registered where I was going – until I reached the turn off for our jetty.

What *used* to be our jetty.

It couldn't be further from a place I recognised as home now. Mind you, the place that apparently *was* my home now was beyond recognisable too. *Nothing* was the same. I was about to turn away when I noticed a figure at the far end of the jetty, making their way towards the fancy yacht at the end. Even in this dim light, I recognised that walk.

Mr Beeston.

What was *he* doing here? Was he visiting someone? Who could he possibly know that lived on a yacht like that? There was only one way to find out. I'd have to follow him. There was just one problem. The entrance to the jetty was locked.

I went over to the gate to see if there was an intercom system or something. It had a screen like the one at school. The moment I looked into it, the screen burst into life with a picture of me! Thirty-three-year-old me.

Then the gate opened.

Why was it allowing me in? Was our boat still here somewhere after all, hidden behind the super-yachts? A shiver of nerves ran through me, along with a trail of questions. What was I going to find down here? What was Mr Beeston doing here? What was *I* doing here?

The last one was easy. I was here for one simple reason.

I needed some answers.

'Emily! How nice to see you. Are you coming aboard? Mum'll be back soon.'

Mr Beeston was grinning at me from the deck of the shiny yacht, reaching his hand out to help me aboard as if it were the most normal thing in the world.

He didn't look all that different. His hair was a bit wispier, combed sideways across his head; his face was wrinkled. But other than that, he looked pretty much like the same Mr Beeston I'd known all my life.

I clambered on to the boat. Mr Beeston leaned over to kiss me on the cheek and I involuntarily shrank away from him.

What was he doing that for? *Ewww.*

He recovered quickly, reaching over to check one of the ropes on the boat instead. Then he beckoned me towards the door. 'Come on, I'll get the kettle on and you can tell me all about your day,' he said.

Tell him all about my day? Tell him what? That it started almost exactly where we were standing now?

Except I was on a very different boat, I was with my mum and dad – and I was thirteen years old?

'Oh, you know, same old, same old,' I said.

I followed him inside the boat. The inside took my breath away even more than the outside. Everywhere I looked it was all polished wood, shining metal, expensive-looking furniture.

'Wow,' I said, before I could stop myself. 'This is nice.'

Mr Beeston swung round. 'What's that?' he asked.

'This place,' I said.

He gave me a strange look. 'We've lived here for nearly nine years,' he said.

We?

Who was 'we'? I didn't want to ask.

'I, um, I mean it's looking very tidy today. Today. Right now. Tidy and clean,' I blustered.

Mr Beeston went back to making tea in the galley. 'That's your mother for you,' he said over his shoulder.

WHAT?

What did he just say? What did he *mean*? My mum was Mr Beeston's cleaner?

But even as the thought came into my head, I noticed something across the room. A photo in a frame on top of a dresser.

I crossed the room and picked it up. My hand shook as I held it.

Mum and Mr Beeston, standing on the deck of

this boat, smiling at the camera. They each held a champagne glass in one hand.

With their free hand, they clasped on to one another.

Mum and Mr Beeston?

I hadn't heard him come back in the room, but a moment later he was beside me.

'Ah, happiest day of my life,' he said. 'I've been looking at anniversary gifts today, as it happens.'

Happiest day of his life? Anniversary gifts?

Suddenly there wasn't enough air in the boat. I could barely breathe.

Mr Beeston was holding out a cup of tea for me.

'Sorry,' I gasped. 'I can't stay.'

'Are you all right?' he asked. 'You look quite pale.'

'No honestly, I'm fine,' I said, trying my best to give him a reassuring smile, although my jaw was so tight it probably looked more like I was snarling at him. 'Just remembered I have to do something. Year Nine. Homework.'

I crossed the room as quickly as I could. Mr Beeston followed me to the door. 'I'll tell your mum you called by,' he said.

'Yes. Yes, do. Thanks. Bye.'

And before he could say anything else to turn my already distorted world any more upside down, I jumped off the boat, waved goodbye and left.

As I walked along the shiny boards of the pier, I barely even knew where I was going. I let my feet take me and I kept my mind as empty as possible. I didn't want to look too closely at what was in there.

Which was how I nearly walked off the end of the pier.

It was almost dark by now. The water swirled around like a moving shadow. Occasional glints of white as the water broke against the struts of the pier. There was no moon.

Just darkness. And me.

I had no idea what to do. I couldn't go back to the boat; I couldn't bear to see Mum with Mr Beeston. I couldn't go back to Shiprock and deal with Shona's disappointment. And I couldn't go back to that fancy soulless apartment that had nothing in common with my life. I had nothing and no one and nowhere to turn.

Unless . . .

Was my dad out there somewhere?

I stared at the sea, willing it to answer me. A wave broke against the jetty in reply, splashing my feet.

It was worth a try. I couldn't think of anything else.

So I crept down the steps in the darkness and jumped into the cold, dark, deep blue of the sea.

I'd been swimming for hours and I was totally lost.

Nothing was the same as I knew it, either on land or in the sea. Everywhere I went it was unfamiliar and scary – and I was stuck here. My tears mingled with the seawater and blinded my vision.

'Emily?'

Who was that?

I swiped my hand across my eyes and peered into the murky darkness. A face. A pair of eyes. A smile I knew so well.

'Dad?'

I rushed so hard into his arms he swam into a backwards somersault.

'Hey, little 'un! I haven't had a greeting like that in some years,' Dad said, laughing as he righted himself.

Little 'un. He still called me that!

'How did you know I was here?' I asked.

He nudged a thumb behind him. 'One of Neptune's guys thought he saw you and gave me a shout. What are you doing out here at this time? Long way from home, aren't you?'

He had no idea *how* far from home I was.

'I wanted to see you,' I said simply. I studied him as I spoke. His eyes had fans of lines around them. His head had less hair. But his face was the face I knew and loved so well.

'Come on, let's go back to my place,' he said.

I swam alongside him, not caring where we went as long as I was with him.

'How's your mum?' he asked.

How was I meant to answer that? *Oh, you know, she seems to be married to the guy who spent twelve years drugging her with iced buns and spying on us both and then pretended to be your friend.*

Dad registered the look of panic on my face and must have taken it for something else.

'I know, I know,' he said. 'I'm not meant to ask you about her. You hate being in the middle.' He stopped swimming and looked intently into my eyes. 'We still care about each other, me and your mum,' he said. 'We always will. Whatever we managed to do wrong we did one thing right, and that was you.'

Could I risk a question?

The words came out before I could stop them. 'What happened, Dad?'

He turned away and started swimming again. 'Yeah, I ask myself the same thing every day. But you know, it's for the best. It was hard enough holding things together even when life was good. But when those Midas people wrecked the ocean and Neptune went to war with humans again, well, it was impossible.'

Neptune went to war with humans?

'Did he actually go to war?' I asked.

Dad laughed. 'It's just an expression. Not exactly war. But you're right – not far off. We had to pick sides back then, didn't we? And I don't blame your mum for choosing the winning one. Or you. I know you tried to build bridges for a good few years.' Dad sighed. 'Some worlds are too far apart to stretch a bridge over. If you try, it'll collapse and you'll fall through the middle.'

I was about to ask more. I was *desperate* to ask more. But then Dad said, 'Anyway, let's not rake over the past, eh? We're where we are now and we have to make the best of it. Now, tell me about the first day back. Usual mayhem?'

We swam side by side. I told Dad a few things about my first day back at school. I just switched the details so he wouldn't know I was describing my actual first day, and would think I was giving the teacher's point of view instead.

He laughed and listened and asked questions, and soon we'd reached a row of caves lined up along the seabed. Dad swam into the first of them.

It had a trident over the entrance. Neptune's signal. I guessed this was where Neptune's team lived. I followed Dad inside and had to bite on my hand to stop myself letting out a sob.

It was like an underwater bachelor's pad. Or like the prison cell where I'd first seen him: stony furniture with Dad's stuff on it; a single bed in the corner; a kitchen of sorts.

A photo of me, Mum and Dad together was pinned on the rocky wall. It had a waterproof seal around it, but looked like a regular photo. I didn't look much older than I was now – than I *felt* now. We were all smiling.

I swam over to look at it more closely.

Dad saw me looking at it. 'Love that photo,' he said sadly. 'Those days seem like a lifetime ago, don't they?'

I didn't know how to answer him. I didn't know how to answer any of this. And suddenly I felt too tired to even try.

'Dad, can I stay here tonight?' I asked.

'Sure you can.' He pointed to a hole that led to another section of the cave. 'Spare bed is always ready for you, little 'un. You look tired. Why don't you go off to bed now? I'll wake you up bright and early for work in the morning.'

I swam over to him and kissed his cheek. Then I swam through to where he'd pointed, into a tiny cave with a low rocky wall and a stony bed in the far corner.

I hadn't often slept underwater but I knew I could. In fact, as I stretched out and yawned, I realised I was so tired I could probably have slept standing up.

I lay down on the stony bed and pulled the reedy blanket up to my chin. As I lay down I felt something fall from my pocket. Fumbling around, I found the stone. Despite everything, it felt warm and comforting in my hand. I closed my fingers around it and tried to switch off my thoughts.

It wasn't easy. My brain felt as if it were swimming with everything that had happened. All the conversations were playing and re-playing in my head, overlapping and criss-crossing, looping in and out and around each other. Every bit of me was completely exhausted: brain, body, spirit. Everything. I had never felt so drained. My eyes closed and I felt my body shut down.

The thoughts faded away and the day drifted from me as I fell into a twitchy troubled sleep.

The dream came over me like a fierce tidal wave.

The current had me. It was stronger than anything I'd ever felt. Stronger even than the flow that had pulled me under the falls at Forgotten Island. Stronger than the tide that had dragged me to Halflight Castle. Stronger than anything. It was stronger than me, too. I couldn't fight it. I swam as hard as I could but nothing was working.

I tried to call out. I could feel my mouth moving – but my screams were silent. My voice was locked inside me.

I had to wake up.

But I couldn't. Sleep pressed me down as heavily as the current.

Panic was rising. I could feel it run from the top of my head to the tip of my tail.

My tail.

Of course! I was a mermaid. I could swim against this. I *had* to.

I flicked my tail as hard as I could – but it did nothing.

Eventually, I gave in to the force of the water. It took hold of me, grabbing me, clutching me so hard I felt as though a giant had taken hold of me and curled his hand around me. The current spun me into a ball and hurled me about, like a rag doll in the fastest spin-wash in the world.

Frothing angry water everywhere. I couldn't see. I couldn't speak. I couldn't fight it.

I had no power left. Nothing to give. Nothing to offer.

I had nothing.

I gave up. I let the force take me. Let the current do what it wanted with me.

You win, I thought, *you win*.

CHAPTER 10

I woke with a start. Where was I?

Oh yes, I remembered now.

I remembered everything, even if I wished I didn't. I was in Dad's cave, in his spare room. On a rocky bed.

Strange. It felt more comfortable than a rocky bed. I turned over and started to fall asleep again. It was so cosy, I didn't want to get up.

Wait.

Cosy?

I opened an eye. I wasn't in a cave. I was . . .

I leaped out of bed. Bed! *My* bed!

I was in my bedroom! On *Fortuna*, our boat! I was home! I ran to the mirror on my wall, peering in it to check I was right. Yes! It was me! Thirteen-year-old Emily.

I reached up to touch my face as I stared at it. My skin felt familiar. Younger again. I looked around my bedroom. Yes. It was all the same. Exactly how I remembered it.

I looked back at my reflection. My hair was tousled, cheeks creased from sleep.

I'd been asleep. Of course! It was a dream! I must have fallen asleep ... but when? I couldn't remember. Who cared?

I couldn't wait to tell Mandy and Shona. Not just that I'd had such a vivid dream, but that I'd thought it was real! How ridiculous, thinking I'd gone forward twenty years! I lay back down on my bed, almost breathless with relief. A dream. Nothing but a—

'Wakey, wakey!' Mum's voice called from outside my bedroom.

'Rise and shine!' she added as she tapped on my door. She poked her head round the door. 'Come on, up you get.'

'I'm awake,' I said. I was about to tell her about my crazy dream when Mum sat on the end of the bed and smiled. 'Back to school! Are you excited?'

'Huh?' I said. 'That was yesterday, wasn't it?'

Mum laughed. 'I'll get you some breakfast,' she said. 'Hurry up, now. You don't want to be late on your first day back.'

Then she got up and left me to get dressed.

Mum closed the door and I sat up in bed. My body turned cold with recognition and fear as I replayed the conversation in my head.

There wasn't anything particularly strange or unusual about it. But there *was* something scary about what Mum had said.

It was *exactly* what she'd said to me yesterday too.

My heart was fluttering as I went to join Mum in the saloon. I sat down at the table and looked at my breakfast: poached eggs, sausages, bacon and a crispy hash brown.

Exactly the same breakfast she'd made for me yesterday.

I could almost feel my throat close up as a sense of panic began to wriggle through me. It felt like a snake made of ice was slithering around my body.

Mum saw me looking at my breakfast. 'Back to school treat,' she said with a smile.

I tried to make my mouth smile back. I probably looked like one of those super-scary clowns with a massive painted-on grin. 'Thanks, Mum,' I managed to say.

But I couldn't eat. I could barely breathe.

What was happening?

'Come on, love,' Mum said. 'Eat up. You'll be late.'

My stomach felt as if it had frozen over. I remembered her saying the same thing to me yesterday. *Exactly* the same thing.

'I – I'm too nervous to eat, Mum,' I said. At least that much was true. Mum must have assumed I meant because of it being a big day. I was pretty sure I'd said the same thing yesterday.

'OK, chicken,' she said. 'I'll give it to your dad. He never turns down a hearty breakfast.'

If I remembered rightly, in a moment she'd pull her dressing gown around her, go to the fridge and tell me to at least take some fruit with me.

Mum pulled her dressing gown around her and went to the fridge. 'At least take some fruit with you,' she said calmly. Naturally. As though this weren't the freakiest thing that had ever happened to me in my entire life!

'I – I will,' I said, parroting what I remembered saying last time. I felt like I was in a play, remembering lines that didn't mean anything to me, lines that weren't really about me – but I was saying them anyway because the people around me expected to hear them.

Feeling like a wooden doll, I got up from the table and went to the bathroom to brush my teeth.

Then I went back to my bedroom to get my school bag and make my bed.

As I pulled back the duvet, something fell on the floor. I bent down to pick it up.

The wishing stone. I'd fallen asleep holding it.

As I turned it over in my hands something scratched at my thoughts. A memory of something that might give me a clue.

The poem that had come with it.

I grabbed my school bag and dug around for the poem. Opening it up, I scanned the lines.

Make your wish and make it fast.
But don't expect your dreams to last.
Hurry up now, time won't wait.
Slip through worlds and meet your fate.
When you have a magic stone,
Hold it close to take you home.
Life will never be the same
Once you've looked through its dark frame.

When I'd first read it, I'd brushed it off as some kind of nonsense poem. Reading it now, it didn't seem like nonsense at all. The stone had answered my wish and then taken me forward to show me the consequences. I'd slipped through worlds and met my fate.

I'd seen an awful future. Was that what it meant by 'the stone's dark frame'?

And I'd held the stone close as I'd gone to sleep.

Had it brought me home?

My head was starting to hurt from the thoughts beating around in my brain. I had no way of being able to find any answers. I could barely even form the questions.

I folded up the poem and put it and the stone in my jacket pocket. Despite everything, I felt safer having them near me than leaving them behind. Then I shook away all my questions and thoughts and carried on getting ready for school, my mind blank, my body going through the motions like a puppet on a dark, lonely stage.

Mum came out on to the deck in her dressing gown.

'Have a good day at school, darling,' she said. She leaned over to give me a kiss. I climbed off *Fortuna* as though I were in a dream.

Could *all* of this be a dream?

'Thanks Mum,' I said as I stumbled on to the jetty. 'Have a good day too.'

I was about to turn away when I spotted Dad swimming around the back of the boat.

Dad! They were here, together. A tiny bit of my heart unclenched.

'Hey, little 'un. Today's the day,' he said, exactly like he'd said yesterday. He wiped a strand of hair off his face. 'It'll be wonderful, I'm sure.'

What could I say? *Actually, Dad today isn't the day. Yesterday was 'the day'. Today is the day after the day. Today is the day when the world around me has turned into something in between a freak show and a horror movie.*

Somehow I didn't think that was what he wanted to hear.

'Thanks, Dad,' I said instead. I felt as though I were having an out of body experience. As though the real me was in there somewhere while I watched an imposter take over my body and speak words that everyone around me was expecting to hear, instead of the ones that I really wanted to say.

So I blew my parents a kiss, hitched my bag over my shoulder and made my way up the jetty.

'Come on now, 8P. Let's settle, down shall we?'

Mrs Porter shuffled papers around on her desk while most of the class carried on chatting, emptying bags, teasing each other and swapping gossip.

I had nothing to say. I stared ahead of me, letting it all happen around me as if I were watching it from the other side of a glass partition.

I didn't care that no one was talking to me. I didn't bother trying to look busy. I barely even noticed the smiles, laughs and whispered gossip. I didn't want to be part of it.

Aaron's empty seat was on my right, as blank and alone as I felt.

Mandy pulled out the chair on my left, shoved her bag under the table and sat down.

I didn't even turn in her direction. I knew she would ignore me so why bother? I didn't nudge her, I didn't say hello. I didn't want to see her scowl at me in reply.

Even so, from the corner of my eye I noticed her turn completely away from me. She did it so pointedly it was hard to miss. And yes, it felt like a stab in the chest. Just as it had felt when she did the exact same thing yesterday.

Mandy talked loudly with Julie Crossens. I had a second of wondering if maybe it was for my benefit. If she were trying to make me jealous. Trying to get a reaction. But I couldn't react. I was numb.

'Come on guys, enough's enough,' Mrs Porter said. Eventually, everyone hushed.

'Thank you,' she said. 'OK, come on, let's use our registration time to do some catching up. I'm going to call on each of you one by one to tell us your favourite thing from the winter break. And I hope you all had a more interesting time than I did!' Mrs Porter smiled as she glanced around the class.

At least I was prepared this time. I just wanted to get my turn out of the way and then retreat into the shadows.

I put my hand up.

'Yes, Emily.'

'My favourite bit was staying up for midnight at New Year,' I said. 'We listened to Big Ben on the TV and we all sang songs and then went outside to watch the fireworks.'

The lie slipped off my tongue so easily.

'That sounds lovely, Emily. I watched those fireworks too and thought they were incredible!' Mrs Porter spoke so warmly I felt my cheeks flush. 'OK, anyone else?'

Sherry Daniels put her hand up. 'I went out fishing on my dad's boat,' she said.

'Sounds good,' Mrs Porter said. 'Catch anything interesting?'

Sherry shrugged. 'My dad caught loads. I mainly just helped with the ropes and tried not to be sick.'

Mrs Porter laughed. 'Who's up next?' she asked.

Every word turned my insides colder and colder. Next it would be Tammy Bayfield. Right on cue, Tammy put her hand up. 'The newspaper closed for Christmas,' she said. 'So I got to hang out with my mum every day.'

'Good for your mum,' Mrs Porter replied. 'We all need a bit of time off over Christmas!'

Now it would be Aiden Harris, the boy whose dad owned the local tip.

Aiden thrust his hand in the air. The words burbled out of him, just like yesterday. 'My dad took me for a ride in the tipper truck on Boxing Day,' Aiden said. 'We sat in the truck together on the harbour and looked out to sea. Dad wanted to see a dolphin. He's lived by the sea all his life and never seen one. He says it's his biggest dream. We didn't see any dolphins, but I still had a great day hanging out with my dad.'

Succinct as always, Aiden, I said under my breath at the same time as Mrs Porter said it out loud.

Just like yesterday, she went around the whole class. At least this time I'd got my turn out of the way straight away.

And at least I knew what was coming when Mrs Porter asked Mandy to share her favourite part of the holidays and Mandy said, 'My favourite thing in the holidays has been hanging out with my best friend.' I looked down at my desk so I didn't see her give me a pointed look before adding, 'Julie. The *best* best friend in the world.'

Being ready for it didn't make it hurt any less. If anything it felt even worse hearing it a second time.

As soon as Mrs Porter had dismissed us I left the class and hurried down the corridor. I knew from last time that I could get away with missing PSHE. But I didn't go to the nurse this time. I went to the toilets. I checked all the doors. Good. I was alone.

I went inside one of the cubicles, sat down, put my head in my hands, and cried.

I didn't move till the bell rang for the end of first lesson.

'You can get through this,' I said aloud to my reflection. 'You can make things right with Mandy. You are Emily Windsnap, you've been in worse situations than this.'

My reflection frowned back at me. It wasn't convinced, and nor was I.

Still, I couldn't hide in here for ever so I washed my face, took a deep breath and went to join the others for English.

We were following along in our books as Miss Westfield read a passage from Year Eight Comprehension Tests.

The teacher was looking at her book; everyone else was looking down at their own.

I knew what I had to do.

I pulled out my jotter, quietly tore off a page and scribbled a note.

Mandy. I need you. Something awful has happened and you're the only person I can talk to about it. Meet me at lunchtime at the end of the school yard, and I'll tell you everything! Please?

I nudged Mandy and shoved the note to her under the table.

She took it from me and read it. Finally she scribbled something on the bottom of my note and passed it back to me.

I read the note. Seven words.

OK, but it had better be good.

Finally I let myself smile. I had till lunchtime to work out what to say. Two hours to work out a way of condensing the craziness of my last twenty-four hours and find a way to explain it to Mandy. Then I just had to hope she'd believe me and want to be my friend again so we could figure out what the heck had happened to my life.

It wasn't going to be easy.

'*Seriously?*' Mandy burst out. We were in our place in the school yard and I'd told her everything. It hadn't exactly gone well.

'That is the best you can come up with as a way of us making friends again? Some bonkers story that you expect me to believe?'

'I promise it's true,' I insisted. 'Every word of it.'

Mandy puffed her cheeks out and looked away. I

held my breath while I waited for her to say something else.

Finally she turned back to me and shook her head. 'Sorry, Emily,' she said. 'I thought you genuinely wanted to get us back on track. I even let myself think it might be nice, thought it might be like the old days; you and me dead close again.'

'I *want* it to be like the old days,' I said, my voice starting to crack as tears filled up my throat. 'I want it more than anything. Mandy, I promise I'm telling you the—'

'I'm not going to be made a fool of,' Mandy cut in. 'I've got other friends. I just don't need this. First you disappear for months, don't include me in your adventures. Then you come home and spend the entire holidays with Aaron.'

'He was going away!' I protested. 'It was our last few weeks together.'

Mandy carried on as if I hadn't spoken. 'And then you make up one of the most ridiculous stories I've ever heard – even for you!'

'Mandy, it's not ridic—'

'Sorry, Em,' she said, holding up her palm to stop me. 'We're done, I'm out. I need some normal friends – and some loyal ones too.'

Before I had the chance to say anything else she'd turned and walked away, leaving me feeling more lonely and lost than I had ever felt in my entire life.

CHAPTER 11

I honestly don't know how I got through the rest of the day.

If you had asked me what lessons I went to, who was sitting where, what anyone said, I wouldn't have had a clue. I went through it all like a zombie.

Finally the bell rang for end of lessons and I was out of school like a shot. I couldn't bear to spend a second longer in that place than I had to.

As I made my way across the school yard, I saw Mandy and Julie hanging out together at the far end. I was crossing the yard a minute or two earlier than I had last time, so it was only the two of them for now. Aiden and a couple of the other boys were ambling over to join them. I could hear them talking as I passed them.

'You coming to football practice on Friday?' one of the boys was asking.

'Can't, sorry. Mum says I've got to go straight home from school on Friday, as we're having early tea,' Aiden replied.

I was about to switch off and hurry away when he added, 'Dad's got some stupid meeting later in the evening. Something about gold. King Midas or something.'

What?

Aiden's dad was planning to go to the Midas meeting?

I had almost reached Mandy and Julie. Should I tell Mandy about it? Would she listen? Did I even *want* to? Look what happened last time!

As I approached them, Mandy turned away from me. Well, that was my cue. Forget it. All it did last time was make everything worse anyway. I left them to it and didn't even bother trying to speak to Mandy.

As I ambled through the streets alone, taking the long way home, I tried and tried to get my head around everything.

I couldn't. In the end, I headed back to *Fortuna*.

Only Mum was out. Yeah, that made sense. I was home later than I'd been yesterday, so she'd probably already gone to the shops. The boat was locked up and I didn't have my key. It seemed like today was destined to get worse and worse.

As I stood on the jetty, trying to decide what to do, I knew there was only one thing I really wanted to do, only one person I wanted to see and one place where I might get another chance of putting this day right again.

I got up, brushed myself down and hurried to the end of the pier, my spirits lifting with every step.

Shona would be pleased to see me. Shona would welcome me and want to hear about my day. Shona would believe me when I told her things that no one except a best friend would believe.

At least I hoped as hard as I've ever hoped anything that she would.

As I swam, my desire to see Shona kept on bumping into something else: the memory of what it was like last time I was with her. The future version of Shiprock – and the future version of our friendship.

What if it happened again? What if it was already like that *now*?

I didn't think I could take it if I lost Shona again. I wouldn't have anything left to hope for if Shiprock was destroyed.

The closer I got, the more everything became mixed up in my head. The past, the present, the future, Shiprock, Brightport, Mandy, Shona, me. Around and around it swirled in my head, frothing and bubbling like the wildest sea.

Stop!

I couldn't do it. I couldn't leave it to chance.

I stopped swimming. Treading water with my tail, I reached into my pocket and pulled out the wishing stone. As I held it in my palm, it seemed to calm me. Its warmth spread through me. The second line around its middle was shining.

Could I?

Look what had happened last time I'd made a wish. How badly everything had gone wrong.

But the stone felt so warm and comforting in my hand. Surely I couldn't blame the stone for what had happened in the future? It was humans who had messed things up, not the wishing stone. Maybe I could use the stone to help prevent that happening again? And protect my friendship with Shona at the same time!

Before I could talk myself out of it, I held the stone in front of me with both hands. Then I whispered, 'I wish that humans won't destroy the sea. Please let Shiprock, Shona – and our friendship – stay intact.'

In reply, the stone immediately warmed up so much my palm felt hot. Just like last time, it began to buzz and vibrate. The stone had heard me. It would do it. I knew it would.

The relief I felt was like a physical weight being taken off me. I swam on, lighter, happier and freer than I'd felt all day. I barely made any effort, barely noticed where I was going, barely cared.

Which was why I was already being swept away by the tide before I realised what was happening.

NO! Not again!

Bubbles and froth surrounded me, like last time. And the force tugged at me. To begin with, I didn't try to fight it. At first, I told myself it was just a normal current and it would ease off soon. But as the current grew, I felt the stone heat up in my hand and I knew this wasn't a normal current. It wasn't a rip tide. It was the stone, propelling me forwards again.

By the time I'd faced up to what was happening it was too late. I was in the current and it was pulling me so hard that getting out of it felt about as likely – and as dangerous – as jumping off a speeding train.

I tried to fight it, flicking my tail as hard as I could and working my arms till they burned. But even as I fought it, I knew I was wasting my energy. The stone buzzed and tingled in my hand. I couldn't let go of it. It was as though it had an engine inside it, pulling me on and on.

I tried not to think too much. For one thing, if I focussed on what was happening I'd start to panic, and that was the worst thing I could do. But there was another reason too. One that I didn't want to look at too closely.

A small bit of me *wanted* this to happen. A part of me couldn't help being curious. Somewhere amongst the fear and the anxiety and the panic, a tiny corner of my brain wanted to know: would it all work out this time?

Whatever I was thinking – or not thinking – suddenly became irrelevant, as the current turned into a rollercoaster and all I had left was panic.

No. No. Please no. I didn't want this, I couldn't go there again. How could I have thought even for a millisecond that I wanted to go through this again? I didn't. I couldn't. I wanted to get off.

But there was no getting off this ride. The force tipped me downwards and hurled me towards the seabed. Down, down. On and on.

A rumbling sound echoed through the darkness, just like last time. And then like last time, amongst the dark, swirling, rushing water, a shaft of light appeared ahead of me. At first it flickered and wavered like a candle in the darkness. But as I got closer the light widened and grew stronger.

The stone pulled harder. My stomach twisted and turned. My eyes leaked tears that fell away from me as I sped through the water.

The light grew and grew. And then ...

The seabed opened, and swallowed me whole.

I was in the chasm again.

I felt along the sides of the ridge, staring into the darkness as I swam. The chasm went on and on, twisting through the seabed like a giant snake.

The light was ahead of me, growing stronger and stronger as I swam towards it. I knew from last time that it was my only way out. I just didn't know what it had waiting for me this time.

Then I saw something different.

I'd reached a fork. The main route directly ahead was so dark I couldn't see a thing. To my left, a narrow channel was lit by a shaft of dusty light.

I took the left fork. The stone buzzed gently in my hand.

The effort of swimming became easier with every stroke. A gentle tide was pulling me along. At the same time the chasm began to grow wider again, and lighter. Soon I was whizzing along without even trying and rubbing my eyes against the light. After a while the chasm had grown so wide it had disappeared altogether.

I was in open sea. Clear, bright, sunny, open sea.

Multicoloured fish swam all around me. I'd never seen so many varieties in one place. Six thin silver fish with bright gold fins sparkling in the light swam by in a line. A shoal of green fish with purple fins hovered to my right. A smaller shoal of blue and red striped fish wriggled below me. Ten seahorses danced by in pairs, tails joined as if they were out on a romantic stroll together. I laughed as I watched them.

I swam on. The sea itself felt different. Lighter somehow, as if swimming took less effort. Bluer and clearer too. Everything about it was better than I'd ever known it.

There was something else. I couldn't put my finger on it at first.

It came to me gradually.

The rubbish. The plastic. The mess that humans had made of the ocean.

It had all gone. My wish had come true.

It was easy to get caught up in the beauty around me, marvelling at it all. The colours and varieties of sea creatures filled me with a joy that made me want to laugh.

I wanted to share the feeling. And I knew who I wanted to share it with.

Shona.

As I thought of her, I remembered what had happened last time I met up with her in the future. It was awful. What if it was like that again?

There was only one way to find out. I forced my questions and worries away and swam on towards Shiprock.

I was halfway to Shiprock when I got my first shock. I was swimming past the place that Shona and I called our playground. It was one of the first places Shona and I had ever visited in the sea together. Slides made out of abandoned steel tubes; old fishing nets sprawled across the sand that you swam under; a couple of old discarded bicycles propped up on huge rusty springs.

None of that was here now.

In its place, it looked like a brand new playground had been built. Two gleaming curly tubes stretched almost from the surface of the water, winding round and round to the seabed. A couple of young merboys swam up and dived into the top of the tube as we watched, screaming with laughter as they flew out the other end of it. Their mums were swimming nearby, chatting as they watched their sons. They looked up as I passed.

I smiled nervously at them. One of them gave

me a quick wave. The other said a quick, 'Hey, Emily,' before going back to her conversation.

I swam on through the playground, ignoring the fluttering in my stomach.

Up ahead, the old bikes on rusty springs had been replaced by a giant trampoline made out of a gleaming ship's sail stretched across the seabed and tied on to rocks at the edges. Three young mermaids were bouncing on it, giggling as they rolled upside down, their tails curling around them as they bounced.

Beyond that, a couple of long shiny pipes formed a climbing frame. Next to it, lying in the sand was a boat that looked brand new; it seemed to have been made into an adventure trail. Merkids were swimming in and out of the portholes, chasing each other around it.

Everyone was smiling and laughing. Everything was glossy and immaculate. Our secret playground made of abandoned rubbish had been turned into a gleaming public park.

While no one was looking in my direction, I swam up to one of the bright shiny pipes. A quick glance around me: no one was watching. I calmed my racing heart – and looked directly at the pipe.

My reflection glared back at me. And yes, it was exactly as I'd suspected: once again, I was twenty years older.

I clapped a hand over my mouth so I wouldn't yelp. I didn't want to attract attention.

Then I flicked my tail and slithered away.

I almost couldn't look as I approached Shiprock. All I could think about was how it had been last time I was here: the crumbling rocks, the grimy water, the desolate and destroyed town, the merpeople in rags. Even Shona, unkempt, ruined and angry. The memory made me shudder and I swam with my hands ahead of me, half covering my eyes.

Until I reached the outskirts of Shiprock. Then I moved my hands and stared. I could barely believe it.

Ahead of me, the archway was standing once again – except it was even grander than before. The rocks were gleaming as though they'd just been polished. Sea plants grew in perfect vertical lines up the brickwork, in purple and green and yellow. At the top of the archway the plants had been woven into elaborate ornate letters: *Welcome to Shiprock*.

'Swishy!' I said to myself. I could feel my face widening into a grin.

As I swam through the archway and into Shiprock, relief washed through me. I didn't care if it were the future, the present, the past or what; all that mattered was that everything was fine. Shiprock hadn't been destroyed. It looked more beautiful and cleaner and smarter than I'd ever seen it.

Everywhere I swam it was the same. Caves that used to be dark and narrow had been widened, cleaned, spruced up. Holes had been made in the rocky ceilings so that light fanned through, beaming down on me in warm gold rays.

The wishing stone had fixed things! This time it had made the world right. I couldn't wait to see Shona and make sure it had made *us* right again as well.

I crossed the town square. Last time I was here, merpeople were huddled in dark corners, eyeing me suspiciously as I swam by.

It couldn't have been more different this time.

A group of young mermaids played together, laughing and squealing in one corner while their mums hovered nearby. A couple of older mermen were sitting on rocks outside an entrance to one of the caves. They both had white hair and wrinkled faces, and I guessed they were probably in their seventies. But their wide smiles and their shiny tails and strong muscled arms made them look about twenty years younger.

A group of merkids swam by as I reached the other side of the square. Two mermaids and a merboy. I couldn't help a pang inside me. They reminded me of Shona, Aaron and me. Talking, laughing, hatching plans.

As they passed by I could see the tunnel that led to Shona's home. I swam into it.

As I made my way to Shona's home, I couldn't help marvelling at it all. Even the water felt different. It was so light and clear, it felt like I was swimming through air.

Soon I'd arrived at Shona's cave. I stopped outside, my tail twitching as I plucked up the courage to go inside. I had no idea what might be lying in store for me. But there was only one way to find out.

So I stuck my head inside the door and called, 'Shona! Anyone home? It's Emily!'

CHAPTER 12

For a moment I wondered if I hadn't actually travelled into the future at all, as the mermaid that swam out towards me barely looked a day older than the last time I'd seen her.

It was only when I saw her up close that I could tell that actually she *had* aged – she'd just done it *really* well, like everyone else around here. Tiny little lines stroked the edges of her eyes. Her hair was a shade darker, her tail maybe slightly longer – but her smile was the same.

'Emily!' Shona swam towards me and hugged

me. I hugged her back. I didn't want to let go. We were still friends! I clung to her in relief.

Shona finally pulled away. 'You'd think I hadn't seen you for *years*,' she said, laughing.

'Yeah. Ha, ha!' I replied.

Then she frowned. 'But it has been weeks,' she added. 'To tell the truth, I was beginning to worry about you.'

'Worry about me? Why?'

Shona turned to swim back into her house. I followed. 'Oh, you know,' she said over her shoulder as she swam. 'Same old stuff. The way things are nowadays, especially on land.'

The way things are on land? A knife twisted around in my gut. 'Um. Yeah. They're . . . bad are they?'

Shona stopped and turned. Smiling that same old Shona-smile at me, she said, 'Look at you, still trying to look on the bright side. I admire you for it, really I do.'

Before I could say anything else, she went on. 'I understand, though. I know it's hard for you to get away, with all the rules and regulations. How did you get here? Still got that friendly guard on the west border?'

I had no idea what Shona was talking about or how to answer her. 'Um. Yeah, that's right,' I said in the end.

'It's lucky you caught me. How did you know I was here?' Shona asked.

'You live here!'

Shona stopped swimming and looked me in the eyes. 'Em, are you OK?' she asked.

Could I tell her? Would she laugh at me? Would she believe me?

I couldn't take the risk. 'I'm fine,' I said. 'Why?'

'Because I haven't lived here for over ten years!'

I tried to force out a laugh. I know it probably sounded more like I was choking on a fishbone. 'Yeah. Of course you haven't,' I said. 'I mean you *lived* here. *Lived*. Not live. Just joking.'

Shona laughed too. 'You're so funny,' she said affectionately.

'Yeah. I know,' I agreed. Despite everything I felt better for making Shona laugh. 'So, what *are* you doing here?' I asked.

'Just came over to keep an eye on things while they're away,' Shona replied. Then she laughed again. 'Silly really, when there is a zero per cent crime rate!'

'Wow. Really? That's amazing!' I said. 'So ... things are good, are they? In Shiprock?'

Shona gave me a questioning look before saying, 'Things are really good. They're *better* than good. Things are ...'

'Swishy!' I finished for her.

Shona burst out laughing. 'Hey, we haven't used that old word for ages,' she said. 'You're having a properly nostalgic day today, aren't you?'

'I guess so,' I said. 'So your parents are away, huh?'

'Yeah. Six months now! They've been sending messages with the dolphin post every week but I still miss them.'

I was about to reply but then Shona did something odd. More than odd. *Worse* than odd. Her brow creased and she tilted her head slightly to the side.

'How's your poor mum?' she asked in a weird tone.

'My . . .' I began. I couldn't say anything else. My throat had constricted to the size of a straw.

My 'poor' mum?

'I do think of her often, you know,' Shona went on.

That was when I realised what the weird tone was. Sympathy. I had no idea why. And I didn't have a clue how to answer her. But I knew one thing for sure. I had to find out for myself how my 'poor' mum was.

'Actually I, um, I'm late for visiting her,' I said, dodging the question and at the same time realising how much I meant it. I suddenly had an absolutely burning need to see my mum.

I'd seen Shiprock and everything was great. The world had turned out fine, and my friendship with Shona was intact. I could relax. I could stop being scared.

Now I just needed my mum.

I started swimming back towards the door. 'Sorry,' I said. 'I hadn't realised how late it was. It's lovely to see you. Glad you're well. Got to go. Sorry.'

The words burbled out of me, falling over each other as though they were in as much of a hurry as I was.

Shona followed me to the door. 'It's the spring tide tonight. Will I see you later?' she said as we hugged.

'Um. Yeah, sure,' I said hurriedly. I had no idea where I was meant to be seeing her. I just needed to get away.

'Send my best to your mum, from all of us. Let her know she's in our thoughts.'

I pulled out of the hug and tried to smile. 'I will,' I said.

Shona stayed in the entrance, flicking her tail and waving as I left. 'See you later!' she called.

'I hope so!' I said, finally saying something I knew was true.

With one final smile at my best friend, I turned and swam away from Shiprock and back to my home town, trying my hardest not to worry too much about what might be waiting for me there.

As I swam towards Brightport, I tried to calm the gurgling anxiety turning somersaults in my stomach. I tried to halt the questions doing cartwheels in my mind. I tried to enjoy swimming in the sea, like I always did.

It half worked. The sea was so beautiful it was hard not to enjoy swimming in it. I'd never known it to be like this. The clarity was like glass. The life on the seabed was so colourful it was as if there were rainbows beaming down through the water. The fish that passed swam lazily alongside me, not in any hurry, in a multitude of shapes, sizes and colours. I actually began to enjoy myself.

Then I came into Brightport bay and the somersaulting in my stomach returned.

I swam on, willing myself to stay calm, telling myself everything was going to be fine. Shiprock was so beautiful, *surely* Brightport would be the same.

As I approached Brightport, I swam up, broke through the surface of the water and wiped wet hair out of my eyes. Swirling my tail to tread water, I looked across at the harbour.

My hopes sank like a rock landing with a thud on the seabed.

The thought of a rock made me think of the stone – and with it, two lines of the poem came back to me again.

Life will never be the same
Once you've looked through its dark frame.

Had I honestly thought things would all work out beautifully this time? Or had I just pretended to forget about the stone's dark side and hoped it wouldn't show itself this time?

Either way, something wasn't right in Brightport, and it was too late to do anything other than confront it head-on.

The beach and prom were almost empty. Where Shiprock had been full of smiling merfolk, Brightport had one person walking a scruffy wet dog along the beach and two people scurrying along the prom looking like they were in a hurry to be somewhere else.

I could see why.

The shops along the front looked deserted: half of them were boarded up, the rest had broken windows, peeling paint or dirty guttering. The houses beyond them looked dark and grey. There seemed to be a heavy cloud hanging over the whole town.

I glanced across at the pier. It had almost completely collapsed. The wooden pillars looked like they were mostly rotting. A few of them had come away altogether. One jetty had some half-sunken boats moored alongside it, the rest looked as if you'd be taking your life in your hands to walk along them.

The Rushtons' theme park was still there at the end of the pier, but looked neglected and derelict. I swam closer and could see that all of the rides had yellow tape around them saying 'CLOSED DOWN'.

Did Mandy still live here?

Did *Mum* still live here?

I had to find out. I swam to the end of the pier.

A merman appeared out of nowhere. He had a sleek grey tail and was wearing a smart jacket, a peaked cap and a stern face.

'Documents,' he demanded as he swam towards me. He barely even looked at me.

'Sorry?' I replied.

'Come on, you know the rules. No one comes or goes at the border without the correct documentation.'

I had literally no idea what he was talking about. I certainly didn't have any documentation.

'I – I must have forgotten it,' I said.

The merman looked at me properly for the first time. 'Oh, it's you,' he said. 'Windsnap's daughter.' He glanced furtively around him before waving me on. 'Go on then,' he said. 'Quickly.'

I swam away from the guard and over to the steps at the end of the pier. I followed the line of steps as I wriggled up to the surface, then pulled myself out of the water.

The steps were rusted and they wobbled as I pulled myself up and on to the pier.

Sitting on a rotten plank of wood, I caught my breath and tried not to think about the weird conversation I'd just had while I waited for my body to change.

My tail hardened and stopped flapping. I watched as my legs formed, then my feet. I wriggled my toes to get some life into them. Then I got up and started walking towards the jetty.

The sight made me gasp.

All that remained of the jetty where I'd lived my entire life were a few half-sunken planks of wood and a derelict boat that was barely afloat.

I turned away and made my way along the pier instead, watching my feet with every step. There were planks missing all over the place and I didn't fancy falling through the floorboards and breaking my leg.

I was concentrating so hard on my steps that I barely registered the person huddled in a corner.

Till I heard my name.

'Emily!'

The woman reached her arms out to me as I walked over to her. She was sitting cross-legged at the side of the pier. In front of her, she had a blanket with a crystal ball, Tarot cards, some crystals and a few random objects on it.

'Emily, dearie!' she said, smiling at me. Her teeth were yellow. 'Want me to read your palm? I'll give you a free reading if you like, seeing as it's you.'

I took a step closer towards her. 'Millie?' I asked.

The woman on the floor was dressed just like Millie – in a large cape, with a flowery shawl tied around her neck. She looked almost exactly the same as Millie – apart from the fact that she was about twenty years older than the last time I'd seen her.

And the fact that she was grubby and her shawl was torn and she was surrounded by bags that looked as if they probably contained all her worldly goods.

What had happened to her?

Whatever it was, she didn't seem to mind too much. She smiled at me. 'Yes, lovey. Come on, sit down,' she said, patting the grubby blanket in front of her. 'Plenty of room.'

I crouched down.

'Come on, give me your palm. Let's see if I can read your future, eh?'

I almost choked at her words. Read my future? I was *living* my future.

'You OK there, Em?' Millie asked. 'Got a cold coming on, have you?' She fumbled in a large hessian bag by her side. 'I've got some liquorice root around here somewhere. Have a chew of it, you'll be better in no time.'

'Um. No. Thank you. I'm fine, it's just a tickle,' I replied.

As Millie opened up my palm and leaned forwards to study it, I tried to work out how to ask the right questions to get the information I needed.

'I can see a man here,' Millie said, sounding hopeful. 'About time too, eh?' she added, then burst into a cackling laugh. The laugh turned into a throaty cough and she rolled back on her heels as the hacking went on.

I reached out to pat her on the back. 'Millie, are you OK?' I asked.

She waved a hand as if to swat my question away, then reached into her bag for the liquorice root. 'Good job I've got this,' she said, breaking off a piece with her teeth and chewing loudly.

'Have you seen a doctor?' I asked. 'That cough sounds bad.'

Millie looked at me as if I'd asked her whether she'd been abducted by aliens. 'Seen a doctor?' she asked between mouthfuls. 'What about?'

'About your cough.'

Millie burst into a wheezing laugh. 'You're so funny,' she said in between laughter that turned into a rattling cough again.

'Why am I funny?' I asked.

'I've only had this cough for about ten years,' she said. 'And we have the same conversation every time.' Then she waved a hand towards the town. 'Tell me, my lovely, where do you think I'm going to find a doctor, hey?'

I hadn't been to the doctors all that often, but Mum had taken me a couple of years ago when I was off school with a stomach bug. It was only a few minutes' walk away, on one of the side streets off the prom.

'The one on Park Lane,' I said. 'I'll walk around with you if you like.'

Millie stopped laughing. She stared at me, her mouth wide open. 'Emily, which century are you living in?' she asked.

Good question.

'That doctor shut up shop and left town long ago,' she went on. 'Along with everyone else.'

'*Everyone* else?' I asked.

Millie sighed as she shrugged. 'OK, not everyone else. Bless your mum's heart.'

'My mum?' I felt my *own* heart leap into my throat. 'What do you mean?'

Millie pointed back to where we used to live. The barely standing jetty.

'For staying,' she said. 'You off to visit her now?'

I swallowed – or tried to. My throat was too tight. 'Off to see her?' I asked shakily. I mean – of course I wanted to see my mum. That was what I'd come here for. But Millie was pointing at the boat that looked one step away from being sent to a scrapyard. Was she trying to tell me that Mum lived *there*?

Millie was rummaging in a bag. She scrabbled around for a bit before pulling out a loose tea bag and holding it out towards me. It was covered in crumbs and dust.

I took the tea bag from her, and Millie picked up a grubby plastic cup from next to her on the pavement. She held that out to me too. 'Ask her to get the kettle on, will you? I'd love a cup of Earl Grey,' she said as I took the cup from her.

I stared at Millie. She saw me staring and frowned. 'Come on now, love. Don't be fussing about me. I'm fine. I'm a survivor. Like you and your mum.'

I looked at the objects on her blanket. They each had price tags on them. I was overwhelmed by an urge to help her. I *had* to help her. I couldn't shake the thought that I'd done this to her. My wish had put her here.

'Can I buy one of these?' I asked, casting my eye over the objects.

Millie narrowed her eyes and paused before replying. 'Which one do you fancy, sweetheart?' she asked carefully.

There was a tiny glass jar with a crack on the rim, a bunch of dried lavender, a couple of picture frames and some random animal ornaments. One of them caught my eye. I picked it up. It was an elephant.

'Cute,' I said.

The elephant had a pink trunk, grey feet, blue body, black eyes and a snowy white tail. As I turned it over in my palm the grim daylight caught the elephant's back and, for a brief moment, made it sparkle like a rainbow.

'Can I have this?' I asked, fumbling in my pocket for some change and hoping that they still used the same currency in this world.

''Course you can,' Millie said, with a strange smile. Then she reached out and closed my fingers over the elephant. 'Take it, it's yours,' she said.

'But I wanted to buy something from you!' I said.

Millie made a strange clicking sound with her teeth. 'The day I take money from you will be the day I'm ashamed to be in your life. Please, have the elephant. It's a gift. I insist.'

'Thanks, Millie.' I managed to squeeze the words out past the giant rock in my throat. I had already buttoned the stone into one of the pockets in my jacket. I dropped the elephant into the other pocket.

'You sure you're OK?' Millie asked.

For a split second I nearly told her the truth. I nearly broke down and told her everything. Then I thought again. Millie had enough problems right now. She didn't need me adding mine to them.

'Yeah,' I said, forcing myself to smile. 'I'm fine, honestly.'

Millie looked at me for a beat. Then she seemed to make her mind up about something. 'Hang on a sec.' She scrabbled around in another torn hessian bag on the ground beside her.

I waited.

She rustled around some more, talking to herself as she did. Finally, she nodded. 'Got them!' she said.

Then she took hold of my hand and placed something inside it. 'Here,' she said.

I looked at my palm. Two small pebbles. I looked at Millie. 'What are these?' I asked.

'The stones you told me to give you,' she replied simply.

'Huh? What stones? I don't remember telling you to give me anything!'

Millie tapped her nose. 'Well, it's just as well one of us has a good memory then, isn't it?' she said. 'To be fair, it must have been, oooh let's see, twenty years ago now.'

A shiver ran through me. 'Twenty years ago?'

'Something like that,' Millie said with a sniff. 'You said that I was to keep them, never sell them or get rid of them until the day I gave them back to you. You told me I'd know when it was the right time, and that they belong with the elephant. So please, take them. This is the right time. I can feel it in my bones – and in the cosmos.'

'But Millie, that doesn't make any sense. I've never seen these stones before!'

Millie shrugged. 'You told me that you'd say that as well and that I was to ignore you. I thought you were talking gibberish at the time, but you insisted on it. You said you couldn't explain, but there was too much at stake and I had to promise.' She shrugged again. 'So I did.'

'I …' I began. I had no idea what Millie was

talking about. The conversation she was so certain we'd had simply hadn't happened. It made me sad to see her like this. Her mind and her memories playing cruel tricks on her. Still, I didn't want to make her feel bad about it, so I decided to play along. 'Well, you have a better memory than I do,' I said, forcing a laugh as I buttoned the pebbles into my pocket. 'I'll treasure these.'

Millie waved a hand to dismiss me. 'Go on, off you go. Your mum will be over the moon to see you.'

I leaned forwards to give her a kiss on the cheek. 'I'll see you soon,' I said, so choked with emotion the words came out like sandpaper on a rough surface.

'Oh, go away with you,' Millie said. But her beaming smile told me how much I still meant to her. 'And don't forget my Earl Grey,' she added as I stood up.

'I won't,' I assured her. And then, legs like wood, I got up, turned away and tried to calm my heart rate as I walked towards the rundown barely floating boat that was apparently my mum's home.

CHAPTER 13

*H*ello? Anyone home?'

I stood on my tiptoes on the edge of the jetty and called through a window of the ramshackle boat. The glass had splintered and a corner of it was completely missing. I didn't dare tap on the window in case it broke completely. The door wasn't much better, so calling seemed the best option.

A moment later the tiny hatch-door opened and a face appeared in front of me. A face at once so familiar and so different that I thought my heart might burst right out of my chest.

'Mum!' I practically threw myself through the door and into her arms.

She hugged me with thin spindly arms, laughing as she did. 'What's this for, chicken pie?' she asked.

I drew back from her. 'I'm just so happy to see you,' I said.

She laughed again. 'I'm even happier to see you,' she said. 'I always am. Come on, I'll get the kettle on and you can tell me all about things.'

'Things?'

What things was I meant to tell her about?

'Get me up to speed. Have they given you a day off at last?'

'Something like that,' I mumbled.

Mum pointed at the cup with the teabag in. 'That from Millie?' she asked.

'Um. Yeah, she asked if you could put the kettle on for her,' I said. 'She doesn't seem very well. Bad cough.'

Mum shook her head as she took the cup from me. 'Honestly, the number of times I've tried to get her to move in with me. I wish she would.'

I looked around the tiny boat. It was open plan and only just big enough for a tiny saloon, an even smaller galley, a bed at the far end and what I presumed was a bathroom behind a curtain to the side of the bed. Barely enough room for *one*, never mind two people.

Was Mum 'one' now? I was desperate to know about Dad, but couldn't bear to hear that they'd separated like last time.

I decided not to ask.

The kettle had boiled and Mum was filling Millie's cup. 'I'll just nip out with this,' she said. 'Won't be a minute. Get whatever you fancy, lovey, and make yourself at home.' She stroked me on the cheek as she passed. 'This will always be your home too, you know.'

Once she'd gone, I took advantage of the five minutes or so that I'd have on my own to do a bit of digging around, so I could avoid asking questions like: *Where in fact* do *I live in this world? Where is Dad? And what the heck has happened to everything and everyone?*

First thing I did was grab a newspaper that was lying on the table. It was open on the puzzles page. I smiled to myself. Mum always liked doing crosswords. I was glad to see she still did. The crossword was almost completely filled in.

But it was the news I was after. I unfolded the paper and glanced at the top of the page. The date: yes, it was as I thought. I was twenty years in the future. Again.

I sat down on a rickety chair and started to read. The main headline took up a banner across the page:

Protests as Midas Seals Deal on New Brightport Plant.

Midas were in Brightport in *this* future too? But that didn't make sense. If they'd invested in the town, wouldn't it be full of their glitzy hotels like last time?

I looked at the photo – and went cold inside as I recognised someone. He looked just the same as in the photo I'd seen of him in the other version of the future.

Mr Whittaker. The guy from Midas. So they *were* still involved in Brightport.

Last time I had seen a picture of him, he'd been shaking hands with Mr Beeston. This time he was wearing a hard hat and a massive smile as he shook hands with someone I didn't recognise.

At least, I didn't recognise the *adult* version of him.

The caption read: 'Alan Whittaker and Aiden Harris clean up the details with a new deal for Brightport.'

Aiden Harris? The boy in my class whose dad owned the tip?

A strange cold feeling crept up my spine. Aiden Harris, the boy I overheard telling his mate that his dad was going to the Midas meeting?

Was that who Midas had invested in?

At the edge of the photo there were a load of people holding signs in the air: 'Get your filthy hands out of our town'; 'Houses not Hazards'; 'We Don't Want Your Waste'.

I took a closer look at the photo and at the people holding signs. Right there at the front of them – was Mum.

I read the article.

Brightport residents were out in force this weekend to protest the latest agreement put in place by Midas Waste Management Services.

The new deal gives Midas the right to build a new waste disposal plant at the back of our town. This will be their second hazardous waste site and brings the total number of waste management plants to five.

Mr Alan Whittaker, CEO of Midas Enterprises, told *The Brightport Times*: 'We are delighted to announce this new initiative. Together with Harris Waste Management Company, we are bringing money into the town at a time when no one else wants to. We hope that Brightport residents will see that this move is good for the whole town.'

But the protestors had different views on the agreement. Local resident Mandy Rushton is one of the protest organisers. She said they would take their protest to the courts if necessary.

'Like many others in our town, my family lost everything when visitors to Brightport fell to a level that could no longer sustain our business. Midas are corrupt, money-hungry sharks who don't care about anything except lining their own pockets, even if it means driving our town into the ground.'

The Brightport Times put these claims to Mr Whittaker and he said: 'Midas Enterprises responded to a law that was put into effect almost twenty years ago, banning anyone from disposing of rubbish in the ocean. The ocean looks fine to us. But in order to keep the oceans clean, we have to accept a bit of discomfort here and there. We understand that people are upset, but these protests have a "Not in my backyard" flavour about them. People will always create waste – and it has to go *somewhere*.'

Mr Whittaker added: 'We at Midas have brought more money into this town than any other business in almost two decades. It's time people stopped whingeing and got behind our attempts to save Brightport.'

Meanwhile, *The Times* can report that another seven local firms went out of business in the last month. Brightport's newly elected Mayor, Councillor Windsnap, told *The Times*: 'Midas have once again twisted laws that were set up for the good of everyone, and turned them into opportunities to line their own pockets. Things can't go on like this. We have to stop them. We have to save our town – before there is no town to save.' She added: 'Everyone must get involved.

Come to our public meeting next week. Save Brightport, save our planet!'

See our editor's comment piece on page 12: *Brightport, City of Waste – Where Will It End?*

I folded the newspaper and put it back down on the table. My mind was racing – and so was my heart. It was pumping with fury.

Midas hadn't built glitzy hotels in this version of the future – so they'd looked at another way to make themselves filthy rich instead.

My wish had come true. I wished that we wouldn't destroy the ocean. So Midas were destroying the *land* instead!

In spite of my anger, I couldn't help also feeling proud – Mandy was at the heart of the protests against them. And despite living in a ramshackle little plastic tub, my mum was mayor of Brightport! Still, I couldn't help wondering where *I* was in all of this. It seemed like I had a busy job from what Mum said about me finally having a day off.

Mum was still outside. I looked around the boat to see if there was anything else that might give me clues about life today. There was a dresser along the side of the saloon with three framed photos on it.

I went over to look. I recognised the first picture. It had been taken a few weeks ago on our holiday at Forgotten Island. There we were, Mum, Dad and me, smiling and hugging each other. The photo was worn and faded. In this world, it was a couple of decades old.

The second photo was of Mum and Millie. I guessed that was more recent. They were standing on the pier together. Still smiling, but you could see that joy wasn't filling them up in the same way. Their smiles seemed forced and tired.

I picked up the third photo. Dad. At first sight, he looked barely older than I knew him to be in my old life. He had the same twinkle in his eye he always had – but yes, he had a few lines too, especially around his eyes. He seemed to be upright in the water as I couldn't see his tail. His greying hair was wet and he was smiling and saluting at the camera. He seemed to be wearing a uniform of some sort. What was it? I held the photo nearer and studied it harder.

Just then, I heard Mum on the jetty outside the boat. Still holding the photo, I turned to see her climb back through the trapdoor. She came over and put an arm around my shoulders.

'I miss him so much,' she said.

Miss him? Had they divorced in this world too? Was Dad even *alive*?

My eyes filled with tears and my throat had almost closed up completely when she added, 'At least we get to see him once a month though. You're all set for tonight?'

I swiped my arm across my eye. 'Tonight?'

'Yes! You hadn't forgotten? It's a new moon and I think it's high tide at just before ten p.m. I live for that one hour of the month. And it's even better when I can share it with you. You're coming, aren't you?'

'Of course I'm coming!' I said. I wanted to laugh. I wanted to cheer. Instead I grabbed Mum and pulled her to me. 'I'm so glad you're still together,' I said.

Mum laughed. 'Of course we're still together, silly billy. *Nothing* could come between me and your dad!'

I didn't tell her that there was another version of our lives where that wasn't true. Instead I said a silent prayer of thanks that at least in *this* version it was.

'I just wish we didn't have to have such long stretches apart,' Mum said. 'But in his position, he can't be seen to be breaking the rules.' She pulled me close to kiss the top of my head. 'Still, I couldn't be prouder,' she went on. 'Between my husband as Neptune's new Officer in Charge of Cleanliness and my daughter as the youngest ever mayor of Brightport, I'm thinking we might finally be able to beat those Midas crooks.'

I nearly dropped the photo I was still holding. I put it back down on the dresser before it slipped out of my hands.

What had she said?

Mum wandered into the galley and clicked the kettle on again. While it heated up she came back into the saloon, sat down and patted the seat next to her. 'Now, come and sit down and let's have a cuppa before that phone of yours starts ringing. We've got lots to catch up on. I feel like I've barely seen you since you were appointed.'

I sat down, opening my mouth and trying to make words come out of it. But they wouldn't. The words simply weren't there. I'd read the newspaper article wrongly. Mum wasn't mayor of Brightport.

I was.

My home town was crumbling in front of my eyes; my mum lived on a boat that was barely floating; her best friend was homeless; Mandy's family was ruined. And I was the person in charge. I was the one they were all looking towards to fix it.

I'd faced bad things before. I'd fought off a kraken. I'd swum past hammerhead sharks to rescue my dad from prison. I'd survived an earthquake that had nearly torn an island in two! But for once, I had to admit something I really didn't want to face up to.

I had no idea how to get out of *this* one.

CHAPTER 14

I walked along the pier, thinking everything over. I'd told Mum I'd meet her in an hour and we'd go down to the river together. In the meantime I needed some air. I needed some thinking time. I needed to be alone.

I paced slowly, trying to take in everything that had happened.

But I couldn't. My brain just couldn't process it. Every time I tried to make things right, all I'd done was somehow create a world of horrific inequality. I began to wish I'd never set eyes on that stupid stone.

Except I didn't even dare think about the word 'wish' right now. Who knew what it might lead to?

So instead, I looked down at the wooden boards of the rickety pier as I walked. I hardly even realised where I was going till I reached the end of the pier.

Before I could stop myself, I was knocking on the front door. I shuddered as I remembered what had happened last time I was here. Some girl I'd never seen in my life had answered. She'd been wearing a top that had had a Midas logo on it. It hadn't been Mandy's home any more. It hadn't been *anyone's* home.

I shuddered even more when I thought about my last exchange with Mandy. The one in school this morning.

Had we made friends over the years? Had we grown apart?

I had nothing but questions. Questions and a boarded-up door that clearly no one was answering.

I was about to turn away when I heard the sound of footsteps behind the door. Then a voice. 'Who is it?'

'It's Emily,' I said. *Was that Mandy in there?*

'Emily?'

'Emily Windsnap,' I said.

'Well which other Emily is it going to be?' the voice said. A sarcastic reply that could only belong to one person.

The door opened.

'Mandy!' I exclaimed. I tried hard not to show how shocked I was. Mandy looked like an old lady. Her hair was completely grey. Her clothes looked dirty. Her top had at least a couple of holes in it. But I didn't care. It was Mandy, and I was more pleased to see her than I could express.

I guessed by her scowl, however, that the feeling wasn't exactly mutual.

'What do you want?' she asked, holding the door open a fraction as she screwed up her nose and stared at me.

'I wanted to see you,' I said simply.

'Not too busy then?' she asked.

'I'm *never* too busy to see my friends.'

Mandy snorted in reply. But she didn't turn me away. 'Thought you council folk would be in bed with the Midas crooks by now,' she said. 'Have you not had your backhanders yet?'

'What are you talking about?' I asked.

'You know what I'm talking about, Emily. I'm talking about years and years of having everything you love taken away from you. I'm talking about relying on people who aren't there for you. I'm talking about wondering where your next meal is coming from, wondering who will be next to stab you in the back, who you can trust and who will let you down, over and over again.'

I stared at Mandy. Her words felt like arrows, all aimed at me. I couldn't speak. I could barely think.

'Mandy, have I really done those things?' I whispered eventually.

Mandy ran a hand through her ragged hair and looked away.

'I – look, I should never have come,' I said. 'I'm sorry, I won't bother you again.' I turned and started to stumble away.

'Wait!' Mandy called after me.

I stopped and turned around.

A single tear was running down her cheek. 'I'm sorry,' she said. 'It's not you. I know you've done everything you could. You've probably tried harder than most. It's unfair of me to take it out on you. Just – I'm desperate, you know?'

I closed the gap between us. Standing in front of her, I said, 'Yeah, I know.' And the weird thing was, even though I actually *didn't* know what Mandy was referring to – I didn't know anything that had happened to her for two decades, I didn't know what had happened to our friendship – I *did* know what despair felt like. I knew that *really* well.

'I miss you,' she said, wiping the tear off her cheek.

I smiled at her. 'I miss you too,' I said. 'I never wanted to fall out,' I said.

'Me neither.'

Despite everything, I couldn't help laughing. I had no idea what had happened to Mandy to make her say these things – but she had no idea how much I meant what I was saying in reply.

She opened the door a bit wider. 'D'you want to come in?' she asked.

'I – I can't.'

Mandy's face closed up. 'Thought not,' she said tightly. 'Too busy?'

'No. It's not that. I mean it's not you. It's – I've promised my mum I'll go to the river.'

Mandy nodded. 'Oh yes. It's the new moon. Spring tide. You going to see Shona?'

'I'm going to see my—' I began. Then I remembered Shona mentioning the new moon earlier. Of course. That must have been what she was referring to.

'Mandy, come with me!' I said. 'Come to the river with me.'

'*What*? Why would I do that?'

'Come and see Shona. I'm sure she'd love to see you. She's going to be there. At least – I think she is.'

'She won't want to see me. No one from Shiprock cares about us any more.'

'Mandy, this is *Shona* we're talking about. Come on. When's the last time the three of us have hung out together?'

Mandy let out a bitter laugh. 'You're joking, right? The three of us haven't been together for . . . I don't know. Years. Lots of years.'

'So come with me. Just this once. Let's have tonight. Let's pretend we're all friends like we used to be. *Please.*'

Mandy let out a long, rattling breath. Then she seemed to make up her mind.

'OK,' she said. 'Wait there. I'll get my coat.'

We crept along the bank in the darkness. It was odd. I'd probably been to the back end of town about five times in my whole life – and two of them had been in the future. How was I meant to keep my head straight when it was full of thoughts like that?

'Have you come to the river at new moon before?' I asked Mandy as we walked.

She stopped and looked at me. My eyes had started to get used to the darkness, but not enough for me to read her expression.

'What?' I asked as she set off again.

'We used to come together,' she said. 'Before you were *important.*'

I pretended I didn't hear the sarcasm in her last word.

'Have you changed so much that you don't even remember?'

For a moment I considered telling her everything. Just letting it all out – the stone, the wishes, the travelling in time – all of it. What did I have to lose?

Answer: I had a friendship that was hanging by a thread. *That* was what I had to lose. And it was one of the very small number of things I could claim at the moment, so I wasn't prepared to risk it. Besides, I was pretty sure I could safely say that there wasn't the remotest chance Mandy would believe a word of it.

No, it would only make things worse.

'Of course I remember,' I said instead, covering my confusion with a wave of my hand. 'I meant have you done it *lately*. Since we haven't – seen each other as much.'

Mandy shook her head. 'Not really,' she said. 'There are only two types of people who come here.'

'Two types?' I asked, not looking at her as we walked, and hoping she'd fill in the gaps for me.

'Those with someone to meet, and those rich enough for the black market goods,' Mandy replied, adding bitterly, 'and as you know, I don't fit into either category.'

We walked in silence for a bit. What was there to say? I didn't know what she meant by black market goods, and I couldn't keep asking questions that she expected me to know the answers to. Instead, I watched my feet, plodding along the high riverbank in the darkness.

We soon rounded a bend and I could see a familiar sight ahead of us: the bridge that I'd walked across last time I was here. Mum had already told me that was near where the meetings took place. We'd agreed to meet there.

As we got closer, I could see two groups of people. One looked to be mostly men, mostly in suits, standing in a circle talking rapidly at each other. The other group was made up of individuals, all thin, mostly wearing rags, mostly on their own looking out to sea, none of them saying much. I noticed a couple of them nudge each other and point to me. As they turned to look at me, a few of them gave me a half-smile and a wave. I awkwardly smiled back. A couple of them pulled their ragged coats more tightly around their frail bodies and gave me the kind of look you give to someone who you hold responsible for the fact that your life has fallen to pieces.

'Emily!' A figure from the second group called to me and waved. Mum.

I waved back. 'You coming?' I said to Mandy.

She nodded and we picked our way down to the riverside. As we walked, I said hello to a few people I had never seen before in my life. I guess they knew me – and if I was supposedly mayor of Brightport, I ought to act as though I knew them too.

The river was completely different from last time I'd been here. It was barely a trickle. I could see a tiny thread of water glinting in the darkness. Other than that, the bed looked hard and dry.

We joined Mum and she reached out to hug me. Then she saw Mandy. She paused for a second, then said, 'Come here,' and pulled Mandy in for a hug as well.

Mandy's arms hung by her sides for a moment. Then she put them loosely around Mum's waist.

As they drew apart, Mum studied Mandy's face in the darkness. 'It's nice to see you,' she said. 'Don't make yourself such a stranger. We all need each other in times like these.'

Mandy didn't reply. She looked down at her feet.

Mum put an arm round her, then reached out to put her other arm round me. 'Look at me,' she said. 'Down here at this dried-up river with you two like this. It barely feels like weeks ago that you girls used to play in the water together. What happened to those days, eh?'

I couldn't reply. She had no idea how much I wanted to ask the same thing.

The three of us waited in an awkward silence for a bit. And then it happened.

It started with a sound. A low rumbling, like thunder in the distance.

'Here it comes,' Mum said.

We all moved back to the edges of the river and watched the water flow in.

It was like nothing I'd ever seen before. At first it came in stages, flowing in gradually like a tide normally does. But within minutes the speed increased. It was as if someone had turned on a giant tap to fill the bowl of the riverbed. Water flooded in, raising the level so fast we had to scramble up the bank.

'Catches us out every time,' Mum said, laughing.

I forced myself to laugh back. It seemed like the correct response. But I didn't feel like laughing. I just felt like staring.

Mum saw me watching. 'Never get used to it, do you? The river's spring tide on a new moon. Nature at its most wondrous.'

'Yeah,' I breathed. 'It's incredible.'

In and in it came, flooding in faster than I had ever seen water move. It filled the space so quickly it was like watching someone pour water from a giant jug.

Gradually the river swelled. It reached up the bank and the flow rate began to slow down.

Mandy pointed further up the river. 'They're coming,' she said.

Mum clapped her hands together. 'I see him! I'm going down. You coming, girls?'

I looked at Mandy. She shrugged.

'Sure,' I said.

We scrambled to the water's edge. Further up the river the men in suits were bartering with people in the water. They called to each other, shouting out prices, haggling and jeering, while those in the water held up different items.

'Fish supper for the rich tonight,' Mandy mumbled.

'Fish supper?' I said before I could stop myself. 'They're selling fish to the highest bidder? I'm surprised Neptune even allows it.'

Mandy gave me a strange look. 'Emily, you're acting like you don't even live in this world, like you don't know how it works.'

Tell me about it.

'Neptune's *always* allowed it,' she went on. 'Sure, he *says* he doesn't. But we all know he turns a blind eye, as long as those doing the selling line his pockets along the way.'

'Yeah,' I said. 'Of course.'

'He's here!' Mum exclaimed, and I looked where she was pointing.

Dad!

Yes he was older, yes his face was wrinkled, and yes his hair was half grey and his head was half bald – but the twinkle in his eye was exactly the same, and his smile warmed me up like it always did.

He came straight to us, grabbed Mum and wrapped his arms around her. She giggled with delight like a young girl, not like the older, frailer, ragged woman I'd spent the last hour standing with. Dad brought her alive.

Dad spotted me and swam over to me. I wanted to dive into the water with him but I was nervous. I didn't know the rules of this new world – and there seemed to be a lot of them. What if I turned into a mermaid and it was against the law or something? What if people saw me and – I don't know – what if they did something awful? What if a mayor wasn't allowed to be a mermaid?

I remembered the guard who had stopped me when I was swimming to Brightport. I still didn't know the rules of this world well enough to take risks. So I stayed on the land, even though my heart hurt from how much I wanted to jump in the water and throw myself into Dad's arms.

'Hey, Dad,' I said instead. I allowed myself to tiptoe to the edge of the water and lean over to kiss his cheek.

He smelled of Dad. All salt water and sandy skin. For a second, I closed my eyes and breathed him in.

'How are you?' I asked, through a lump in my throat.

'Oh, you know,' Dad replied. 'Neptune's keeping me busy. You?'

'Oh, you know,' I said, trying to keep my voice light. 'Brightport's keeping me busy.'

Dad laughed. 'So I hear.'

Mandy was nudging me. 'Here's Shona,' she said. I looked where she was pointing.

'Go on,' Dad said. 'Go and hang out with your friends. I'll see you soon.'

'OK. Love you, Dad.'

Dad stroked my cheek. 'Love you too, little 'un.'

I went over to Mum and kissed her cheek too. 'See you soon,' I said, my voice hoarse. 'No matter what, and no matter when, I'll always be here for you. You know that, don't you?'

She looked surprised. 'Of course I do, honey pie. And ditto. Go on, go and see Shona before the tide has turned. You haven't got long. Go and make the most of it.'

I left the two of them, and Mandy and I went over to join Shona. We had an hour to talk. One hour. Would it be long enough for me to figure out what was going on, what had happened to us and our friendships – and the world around us?

I couldn't help thinking I'd need a *lifetime* for that and it still wouldn't be enough.

CHAPTER 15

It wasn't going well. Mandy was her old stroppy self. Shona was trying to be light-hearted and fun. I was stuck in the middle, wondering if all adults acted like this or if there was some way of getting us to be normal with each other.

'So. It's nice the three of us hanging out together again,' I said, trying to sound bright and happy and positive. 'It's been ages, hasn't it?'

'It's been years,' Shona said. 'How are you, Mandy?'

Mandy scowled at Shona. 'You really want to know?'

'I – yes, of course I do. That's why I asked,' Shona replied tightly.

'Well, in that case – I'm pretty dreadful, actually. No, I'm worse than that. I'm barely surviving. I live in a town that's been destroyed.'

Shona looked shocked. 'I know. I'm sorry, I understand that—'

'No, you don't,' Mandy snapped. 'You don't understand *anything* about my life. How could you? Yours is perfect. You have everything you need. Look at you. Your perfect hair. Perfect smile. Even your perfect tail glistens in the dark. Tell me Shona: why do you come here? So you can look at those less fortunate than you and remind yourself once a month how lucky you are?'

'I . . . no,' Shona replied, her voice sounding thin and stretched. 'That's not why I come here at all. I come to visit my friend. My friends. I've offered you my friendship many times. It's not my fault things are like this.'

Mandy made a sneering sound. 'Of course it's not,' she muttered.

I wanted to say something. I wanted to try to get them to stop talking like this, wanted to make them be friends again, but there was nothing I could say.

In the silence, I heard a whooshing sound. 'What's that?' I asked.

'Tide turning. We're running out of time. I need

to start heading back,' Shona said. 'Maybe it's for the best anyway,' she added in a flat voice.

'But we've just got here!' I said.

'It always goes so quickly,' Shona replied.

I looked around. Merfolk were starting to swim away. Mum and Dad were still wrapped up in each other.

We couldn't leave things like this. Maybe I could swim back with Shona. Go back in the ocean, have a bit more time with her.

But then, what about Mandy? I couldn't abandon her now. Not like this.

My head was spinning with so many questions and possibilities that I didn't notice the ground beneath me start to sink. The water was running away from us even faster than it had come in.

A moment later, I heard a yelp. Mandy had slipped and fallen. She was starting to sink into the sand.

'Emily!' she called. It happened so quickly. Before I even registered what was happening, Mandy was flat on her back, being dragged away on the turning tide. Her eyes were wild.

'I'm coming!' I yelled. 'Shona, help!'

Without stopping to think twice, I dived into the water and, with Shona by my side, raced to catch up with Mandy before the tide dragged her out to sea.

I hardly knew what was happening when the rush of water grabbed me, tumbling me over and over.

I lost sight of Mandy in the thrashing, frothing water.

'Help me!' I heard her call. 'Shona! Emily! I'm being washed out to sea!'

'It's just the tide!' Shona yelled as we tried to swim – but mostly got thrashed around like an old pair of jeans in a spin-wash. 'Hold on. We're coming.'

I fought to keep pace with Shona. 'Don't worry Mandy,' I shouted. 'We'll get to you. You're going to be fine.'

I didn't know what made me say that.

Right now I wouldn't put money on *any* of us being fine.

'Wh – what's happened? Where am I?'

Mandy's voice warbled towards me. I wiped hair from my eyes and looked around me. We'd been hurled down the river on the raging tide and out into the open sea.

'Mandy?' I called into the darkness. 'Where are you?'

'I'm – I'm here,' she gasped. 'Help me.'

I swam towards her voice. As I got closer and my eyes once again adjusted to the darkness, I could see her more clearly. Her arms were flapping about, her head slipping under the water as she garbled words. 'Em, get me out of here! Not meant to be here. Not allowed!'

When she re-surfaced, she started coughing and choking.

'Hey Mandy, it's OK,' I said. I reached out to help her stay above water. Her eyes were wild, her legs jerking about so hard under the water she kicked me a couple of times. 'I – I can't be here!' she said. 'It's illegal. I don't even know where I am, how far out we are. Em, there are guards all over the ocean, especially after the new moon. You have to get me out of here!'

I didn't know what to say. I didn't understand anything about this world. I didn't know where we were. I couldn't see the shoreline in the darkness.

What was I meant to do?

A moment later, Shona surfaced beside us. She looked almost as scared as Mandy. Luckily, she had more idea of what to do than either of us.

'Mandy, are you able to swim?' she asked.

Mandy nodded.

Shona turned to me. 'She's exhausted. Let's make sure we stay with her. One on either side. We'll help her find her way. I know where to go. It's not far from here.'

'Where are we going?' I asked.

'Our place,' Shona said.

'Rainbow Rocks?' I asked. 'That's still our special place?'

'Of course it is,' she answered with a new softness in her voice. 'Plus, it's literally the only place I've never seen any guards. It's our best chance of buying some time to think about what to do next.'

'That OK with you, Mandy?' I asked.

'Fine. Whatever,' she said. 'Let's do it. Please, just get me somewhere safe.'

'We'll need to be quick,' Shona said. 'Once the new moon's tide has turned, Neptune will have his rays and hammerheads all over the river. He loves catching humans who break his laws.'

'OK, let's go,' I said.

The three of us swam, Shona and I on either side of Mandy, staying close and slipping through the water as carefully and quickly and quietly as we could.

As we swam, my thoughts felt as dark and blank as the night.

'Thank you,' Mandy croaked, her voice lifeless and dull.

We'd reached Rainbow Rocks and dragged ourselves up and on to one of the smaller, more hidden rocks in the middle.

'You're welcome,' Shona said. 'Don't worry about it.'

Mandy reached out to touch Shona's arm. 'I was wrong,' she said. 'I shouldn't have said those things. I'm sorry.'

Shona put her hand over Mandy's. 'It's OK, honestly,' she said softly.

'I – I just don't know what's happened to my life,' Mandy said in a broken voice.

'I don't think *any* of us knows what's happened to our lives,' I said. It was the truest thing I'd said to her since she'd opened her door to me.

I wished I could think of a way to make her feel better. I had nothing, so we sat in silence for a while, listening to the quiet sounds of the night.

Then, in a whisper so quiet it could have been the sound of a soft wave lapping on the rocks, Mandy said, 'Do you ever wish we could just go back and start again?'

'Back?' Shona asked.

Mandy shrugged and smiled sadly. 'I know. It sounds like a kids' fairytale, doesn't it? Pretending you could close your eyes and make a wish and travel back to a place before any of this happened.'

Something started itching and wriggling inside me.

Shona laughed. 'It's a *nice* kids' fairytale anyway,' she agreed.

But was it? *Was* it just a fairytale? What if it were

possible? It had happened the first time I travelled here. I'd gone back again.

What had the poem said?

When you have a magic stone,
Hold it close to take you home.

Had the stone really taken me home again? And if so, would it do so again?

For a moment, I was filled with hope – till I realised that even if it did work, it wasn't enough. Maybe the wishing stone would take *me* home, but that still meant abandoning my two best friends in this awful world.

Unless . . .

The stones from Millie – were they magic stones too? She'd been so convinced there was something special about them.

'At least we've got our friendship back,' Shona was saying to Mandy. 'And that's the most important thing.'

Yes! Our friendship! I knew *exactly* what I was going to do. It had to be worth trying at least. I opened my pocket and pulled out the two stones. I smiled at my two best friends. Then I held out my hand and opened it.

'Here,' I said. 'These are for you.'

The two of them looked at my palm.

'What are they?' Mandy asked.

I turned to Shona. 'Remember when we were first friends?' I asked. 'We swapped pebbles?'

Shona looked confused for a moment. Then I saw a smile of recognition light up her eyes. 'Our friendship pebbles,' she said. 'Of course I remember. Wow, that's going back a bit.'

I held my palm out to them both. 'Take one each,' I said.

Mandy reached out to take a pebble from my hand. Shona took the other one.

'These are a symbol of our friendship,' I said. 'And a promise that we will *always* be there for each other. Agreed?'

Shona and Mandy caught each other's eyes. Mandy was first to speak. 'Agreed,' she said.

'Agreed,' Shona followed.

I hesitated before continuing. I had to make sure they kept the pebbles with them – but without risking them laughing at the idea that these could help Mandy's wish come true. I guessed that adults in their thirties didn't really believe in magic like that.

I kept my voice light as I went on. 'Keep them close to you *all* the time,' I said. 'As a symbol of our friendship, as a promise that we will always be there for each other.' I looked from one to the other, meeting their eyes. 'Promise me,' I added seriously. 'Keep it with you. Always.'

Shona laughed. 'I promise.'

'Me too,' Mandy said.

'What about yours?' Shona asked.

I pulled the wishing stone out of my pocket. 'I've got this,' I said. 'We all have a reminder of our friendship – and we'll never forget it, right?'

'Right,' Shona said.

'Agreed,' Mandy added.

Shona looked around, peering into the darkness. 'So, what do we do now?'

Mandy's eyes were half closed. 'I reckon I need a rest before we do anything,' she said, stifling a yawn.

'Is it safe?' I asked.

Shona nodded. 'It's the middle of the night. No one will be looking for us here, not at this time.'

I fought down a yawn myself. 'I could do with a bit of a rest too,' I admitted.

'Me too,' Shona agreed, stretching out.

Mandy's eyes had closed completely now. Her fists were bunched up, one of them holding her friendship pebble, as she lay down and curled her legs up to her tummy.

'Look, let's take shifts,' I suggested. 'One of us keeps an eye out while the other sleeps. You go first. I'll look out.'

'You're sure?' Shona asked.

'Yes, definitely.'

'I'll just have a quick nap. Wake me in an hour, OK?'

'Will do,' I agreed.

Moments later Shona had stretched out beside Mandy on the edge of the rock. One hand under her head, the other holding her pebble. Good. Shona's tail flapped in the water; Mandy snored softly as she slept. The water lapped so gently against the rocks, like it always did here. It was making me feel calmer.

And sleepier.

Maybe I could just rest my body a little. I clutched my stone and lay down beside them both. Yes, that felt more comfortable. Just letting my body relax a bit.

Perhaps I could close my eyes. Not to sleep. Just rest.

That was better. I'd lie here for a minute. I wouldn't fall asleep.

I definitely wasn't going to let myself fall asl—

The dream washed over me, blocking out everything else.

I was in a current. It was really strong; *too* strong. Stronger than anything I'd ever felt.

Except – wait. Hadn't I experienced this before? It felt familiar.

Yes, that was it! I'd had this dream before!

A recurring dream. It felt so real.

I couldn't fight the current. I tried; I swam as hard as I could, but it was way tougher than I was. My energy drained out of me.

I tried to call out. Silent screams.

I *had* to wake up. I had to fight it. I pushed hard against it. The current. The sleep. It was closing me in, closing me down.

I flicked my tail.

Wait. Yes, I was a mermaid. And – there was someone else with me now. Calling my name. Two people?

'Emily!'

'I'm here!' I tried to call back. Again, my voice stayed locked inside me.

'Emily!' they called again.

I'm trying to get out.

I tried to flick my tail. Nothing happened.

I was sinking. Lower and lower. Deeper and deeper. Until I stopped fighting.

I gave up. I let the force take me. Let the current do what it wanted with me.

I remember this, I thought. *I remember losing.*

I didn't think anything else. There *was* nothing else. Just darkness.

CHAPTER 16

*B*ANG! BANG! BANG!

I was in a prison cell. They'd caught us.

BANG! BANG!

The guards pounded on the doors as they passed. I put my hands over my ears as they came to mine.

Go away. I just want to curl up and sleep.

BANG! BANG!

'Wakey, wakey!'

'Leave me *alone*!' I cried out.

'Rise and shine!'

Rise and shine? What kind of a guard shouts 'rise and shine'?

'Go away!' I yelled.

A creaking sound. The cell door was opening.

'Come on, up you get,' the guard said.

I turned over in my bed, pulling the pillow over my eyes.

Wait. Pillow? In a cell?

I opened an eye. I wasn't in a cell. And the voice didn't belong to a guard.

'Mum?' I croaked.

Mum sat down on the end of the bed and smiled at me. 'Back to school!' she said. 'Are you excited?'

My whole body turned to ice.

'Am I . . . what?' I asked. My brain felt like mashed potato. Was I really back here again? Back in the present day? The horrors of that future world had truly gone? I didn't dare hope.

I scrabbled around under the sheets for my stone. Yes – it was there!

Had it brought me back home again?

'Mum, pinch me,' I said.

Mum laughed. 'I'll get you some breakfast,' she said. 'Hurry up, now. You don't want to be late on your first day back at school.'

The same words.

The second Mum left me, I leaped out of bed and ran to my mirror.

Yes! I was myself again. I was thirteen-year-old Emily! I pinched my arm. Ow! It hurt! It hurt! I *was* back in the present day.

I had never felt relief like it. Even if I did have to live the day all over again. Right now, I didn't care. I was *me* again. I wasn't in that awful future world. That was all that mattered.

I had the quickest shower ever and went to join Mum for breakfast.

Poached eggs, sausages, bacon and a crispy hash brown. I couldn't help staring. It was the third time she'd made this breakfast for me.

Mum saw me looking. 'Back to school treat,' she said with a smile. Just like last time. And the time before that.

'Thanks, Mum.' I looked at the food on my plate and smiled.

'Come on, love. Eat up. You'll be late.'

I dug into my breakfast. I managed about half of it this time. It was delicious – but I was in a hurry to get away and see Mandy.

'I think I'm done,' I said.

Mum reached over to kiss my cheek. 'OK, chicken,' she said. 'I'll give it to your dad. He never turns down a hearty breakfast.'

Even though I knew she was going to say it, the words still made me smile. Anything that proved I had undone that awful wish could only be a good thing.

I thought of the wishing stone. I still had one more wish. The thought of things going wrong again made my insides turn cold.

I thought of Dad instead. He was still here! They were still together. They hadn't divorced, she wasn't living with Mr Beeston – and they didn't have to settle for a monthly meeting in the darkest night by a raging river.

Mum got up from her seat, pulled her dressing gown around her, and went to the fridge.

I jumped up and followed her into the galley. I knew what she was about to say, and decided to get in first. 'How about I take some fruit with me?' I suggested.

Mum took my plate from me. 'That's just what I was about to say.'

I laughed. 'Great minds think alike,' I said, before going to the bathroom to brush my teeth and get ready for school.

Mum came out on to the deck in her dressing gown. 'Have a good day at school, darling,' she said, giving me a quick kiss.

I paused for a moment. Where *was* Dad? Wasn't this the point where he showed up? My insides curdled. What had happened to him? Had something gone wrong, after all? What if he was hurt? What if I never saw him again? What if—

'Hey, little 'un. Today's the day!'

'Dad!'

Dad swam around the back of the boat and wiped a strand of hair off his face. 'It'll be wonderful, I'm sure.'

'It will,' I said, grinning at him. Then I crouched down and threw my arms around his neck.

Dad laughed. 'What's that for?' he asked.

'Just because,' I said. Then I blew them both a kiss, hitched my bag over my shoulder and made my way up the jetty.

I walked to school as though I were floating on a cloud. The relief of being myself again was enough to keep the smile on my face.

Not that it lasted long.

By the time I reached school, the reality of my life had sunk back in.

Sure, I wasn't thirty-three-year-old Emily Windsnap living in some kind of horrific nightmare future. And no, I wasn't the mayor of Brightport with a town full of problems and no idea how to solve them. And yeah, my parents were still together.

But I was still me.

Which meant I was still sitting here alone with an empty chair beside me and no one to talk to while the rest of the class chattered and gossiped and laughed all around me.

'Come on now, 8P. Let's settle down, shall we?'

Mrs Porter shuffled papers around on her desk while the class ignored her – again.

How many times would I have to live through this? Was this my life now? Was I destined to go through the same thing, over and over again? Survive a miserable first day back at school and then be projected into a nightmare vision of the future. Was that it now? Was that going to be my life: the same thing on a loop, repeating itself over and over again for ever?

I guessed I'd have to live through it at least one more time. The stone still had one more wish waiting for me. Why did that thought make me shudder? Shouldn't magical wishes make you happy?

I gazed ahead of me, staring at nothing. My mind was as empty as Aaron's seat on my right. I couldn't even bring myself to unpack my books or try to look busy.

Even when Mandy came in, pulled out the chair on my left, shoved her bag under the table and sat down, I didn't flinch. I didn't look at her. I didn't want to see the scorn on her face, or watch her gossiping with Julie. I couldn't go through it again.

Except … she wasn't gossiping with Julie. She wasn't talking – to anyone. I glanced at her out of the corner of my eye. She looked as lost and blank as me.

What was going on? This was the bit where she was meant to be making a big show of what a brilliant best friend Julie was. But she wasn't doing that. She wasn't doing anything at all.

The pebbles. The stones from Millie. Had they worked? Had Mandy—

'Come on guys, enough's enough,' Mrs Porter said, just loud enough to be heard over the din. Eventually, everyone hushed.

'Thank you,' she said calmly. 'OK, come on, let's use our registration time to do some catching up. I'm going to call on each of you one by one to tell us your favourite thing from the winter break. And I hope you all had a more interesting time than I did!'

I looked down at my desk, willing Mrs Porter to ignore me, willing myself to turn invisible. My head was filled with only one thought:

Did Mandy's pebble bring her back from the future too?

I was vaguely aware of the other kids sharing their favourite things. Sherry Daniels told us about going fishing with her dad. Tammy Bayfield shared how she'd enjoyed her mum's company. Aiden Harris put his hand up.

'My dad took me for a ride in the tipper truck on Boxing Day,' he said. 'We sat in the truck together on the harbour and looked out to sea. Dad wanted to see a dolphin. He's lived by the sea all his life and never seen one. He says it's his biggest dream. We didn't see any dolphins, but I still had a great day hanging out with my dad.'

'Succinct as always, Aiden,' Mrs Porter said once again.

My insides turned cold and hardened. I wanted to jump up and scream at him: tell everyone what he'd done, or what he was *going* to do, or . . .

Or what? He hadn't done *anything* yet – and in this version of events, maybe he never would.

'Emily?' Mrs Porter was asking.

My mind was blank. I opened and closed my mouth a couple of times – waiting for Mandy to nudge Julie and laugh at me. She didn't.

She was definitely different. I didn't want to get my hopes up. And I couldn't exactly ask her: 'Hey, did you by any chance go forward into a world where you were twenty years older and you'd lost everything – but then find you were back to your normal self when you woke up this morning?'

No, I didn't think that would go down well. But I had to find out somehow.

'Have you got *anything* to share with us, Emily?' Mrs Porter asked.

I had an idea. 'I went to the river with my parents,' I said, my voice quivering as I spoke.

Mrs Porter paused for a moment, as if she was waiting for me to continue.

I glanced quickly at Mandy, then back at the teacher. 'And with my two best friends,' I added. 'It was really nice to hang out with them. Felt like we hadn't done it for *years*.'

My heart was banging like an engine on a tug boat.

'Thank you Emily. That's a lovely memory,' Mrs Porter said gently. 'Now, who have I missed?'

Mandy put her hand up.

I held my breath.

Please don't let her brag about wonderful Julie and their fantastic friendship.

'Yes, Mandy. Tell us your favourite thing about the holidays,' Mrs Porter said.

Mandy didn't speak. She cleared her throat. Opened her mouth. Nothing came out.

'I'm waiting,' Mrs Porter said. Everyone in the class was turning to look at her.

What was going on?

Then Mandy finally found her voice. 'I was given a present,' she said. 'It's not much but it means a lot to me.'

She reached into her pocket and pulled something out. Her hand was closed around it.

'Well, what is it?' Mrs Porter asked. 'I'm sure we're all dying to know.'

Mandy gave me a quick glance. Then she swallowed. And then she opened her hand. 'It's this,' she said. Ignoring the sniggers around her at what she was holding out to the class, she said, 'It's called a friendship pebble.'

Mrs Porter had moved on. She was telling us about the changes to the timetable and letting us know about the new teacher that would be taking our PSHE lesson.

I barely registered her words. I barely listened.

All I could think was: *Mandy still had the friendship pebble. And she made a point of mentioning it.*

Could it mean what I thought it meant? It *had* to. *Surely* it did. I barely let myself hope, in case I was wrong. All I knew for sure was that I had to get Mandy on her own. We had to talk.

When Mrs Porter looked at her watch and said, 'Well, that's all we have time for today,' and everyone leaped up from their seats to file out of the room, I held back in the hope that Mandy would do the same and we could talk.

Julie got in there first. 'Sit with me in PSHE?' she asked.

'Um. Yeah. Sure,' Mandy replied.

Julie was practically glued to Mandy's side as we filed out of the room.

I left them to it and went off to PSHE on my own.

'OK guys, I know it's the first day of term, and we haven't met before, but it's still school and this is my lesson and I would like you all to listen.' Mr Goode, the new PSHE teacher, leaned back on his desk as he waited for the class to hush.

'Thank you,' he said after a couple of minutes. 'Now, today, we are going to talk about a parable. Who knows what a parable is?'

A few of the keen kids put their hands up. As Mr Goode picked one of them to answer, I felt inside my pocket for my stone. Even now, even after everything it had put me through, I still craved the touch of its warm smooth surface.

I'd picked the wrong pocket though. Instead of the stone my hand closed around something small and angular. For a moment, I couldn't think what it was.

I pulled the object out of my pocket to look at it.

'Today's parable is about six men ...' Mr Goode began.

I looked down at the object in my hand.

'... and an elephant.'

What?

I closed my fingers around the elephant in my hand as Mr Goode's voice filtered into my mind, fighting its way past a jumbled mass of thoughts.

'The six men had never seen an elephant. Then one day, it was reported that an elephant had come to their town. They were blindfolded and each in turn was asked to tell the others what an elephant was.'

His voice was soothing and I found myself listening more closely as I turned the elephant over in my hand. Its sides were smooth and cool. Its trunk was pointy and sharp.

'The first man put his hand on the elephant's side and declared that an elephant was like a wall,' Mr Goode went on. 'The second man felt his tusk and told the first man he was wrong, and that an elephant was like a spear.'

I leaned forwards, listening more intently.

'The third man felt the elephant's trunk and said both were wrong and that an elephant was like a giant snake. The fourth grasped a leg and announced that an elephant was like a tree.'

Clutching the elephant in my hand, I focussed on Mr Goode's words so hard it was as if the rest of the classroom had disappeared.

'The fifth man was tall. He reached up to the elephant's ear and said an elephant was like a fan. And then the sixth man clutched the elephant's tail. "You are all wrong," he said. "An elephant is like a rope." The men argued at length, until someone came to them and told them to remove their blindfolds. When they did so, they realised that each of them had been wrong – and each of them had been right.'

Mr Goode stopped speaking. He smiled gently as he looked round at the room. 'Now, can anyone tell me what this story is saying?' he asked.

I didn't even realise my hand had gone up.

'Yes . . .?' he said, looking at me questioningly.

'Emily,' I said.

'Emily, what do you think the parable is telling us?'

I tried to get my voice to work. Nothing came out.

Most of the class were staring at me. 'Want me to ask someone else?' Mr Goode asked.

I shook my head and cleared my throat. Then I answered.

'It's about truth,' I said carefully. 'How – like, there isn't just one version of it. Or, like, one part on its own isn't enough. One person's truth is only part of the story.'

As I spoke, I felt bolts of electricity run through my body. I was almost shaking as I added, 'If you only listen to one side, you won't get the full picture and you can't please everybody. You can only do that when you put *everybody's* truths together.'

Even as I said the words, I hardly registered them. It was as if they came out of my mouth without me even knowing what I was saying.

Mr Goode was beaming at me. 'Beautifully put, Emily. Well done,' he said. 'One philosopher put it like this: "No single truth is ever a complete truth on its own. It is only when we combine *all* our truths that we have a picture full enough to be reliable." I'd say your version is as good as that, if not better. Now, let's have a bit more of a think about this ...'

As he carried on talking, asking questions, setting us a writing task, I was only half there. Probably not even *half* there. Maybe ten per cent of me was in the classroom. The rest of me was in my thoughts, in my head, in the realisation that had slammed into me like a ten-ton truck.

I'd made two wishes. I'd seen two futures. Both times, I'd solved a problem for one side, and made things worse for the other.

I was like a blindfolded man trying to describe an elephant by feeling its tail – and getting it wrong every time. The only way to get it right was if we all removed our blindfolds and figured it out together.

CHAPTER 17

I had to find a way to get Mandy away from Julie.
The lesson had nearly finished so I would have
to be quick.

I tore a piece of paper out of my jotter and
scribbled on it.

Meet me at break? Far end of the schoolyard.

Then I folded it in half and wrote 'Mandy' on
the front. She was sitting on the row behind me,
two desks to the left. I waited till Mr Goode had
turned to write something on the board, then I
leaned back on my chair, gave the note to Harry

Smithfield who was sitting behind me and pointed at Mandy.

'Pass it on,' I whispered.

He took the paper from me, glanced at it and nodded.

Out of the corner of my eye, I watched the note make its way to Mandy. She took it from Hailey Morgan who was sitting next to her.

Please don't reject me. Please don't ignore me. Please don't scowl.

I watched Mandy open the note, find my eyes and give me a quick nod.

Yes!

Feeling slightly calmer, I turned back around to face the front, just as Mr Goode finished writing on the board.

I didn't really register anything else that happened in the lesson. The only thing that was going through my mind was the memory of when Mandy met up with me in the first version of this day, and a silent hope:

Please don't let it turn out like it did that time.

We stood together, huddled at the edge of the yard. I was fully expecting Mandy to sneer at me and ask me coldly what I wanted. She'd done it twice already.

But she didn't react like that this time. Instead, she looked at me with wide, frightened eyes and didn't say anything at all.

'Are you OK?' I asked carefully.

Mandy quickly shook her head. 'No,' she said. 'I'm not OK at all.' Then she paused, and asked just as carefully, 'Are you?'

I shrugged. 'Kind of.'

'Do you know why I'm not OK?' Mandy asked.

I nodded. 'I think so.'

'Go on.'

I remembered last time I'd tried to tell her what had happened to me. The scorn and anger. The disbelief. Could I risk that again? Did I have any other choice?

'What you said in class earlier,' I began. 'About your favourite thing over the holidays . . .'

'What about it?' Mandy asked. She bit her bottom lip while she waited for me to reply.

I took a breath. Then I spoke quickly. 'I gave you that pebble,' I said. 'We got washed through the river then we swam to Rainbow Rocks with Shona. It happened yesterday.' I paused for a second. Then with my heart hammering like a train, I added, 'Or twenty years in the future.' I held my breath and waited for Mandy to reply.

She stared at me for a moment. I readied myself for the onslaught, for the scorn and laughter, for her to tell me to get lost and stop being ridiculous.

None of it happened.

Mandy glanced around and leaned in closer. 'So it *was* real?' she asked in a whisper. 'All of it. It all really, truly happened?'

I nodded, and let my breath out.

'I thought it was a nightmare,' Mandy said, looking at the ground. 'I woke up with a start this morning. Before I opened my eyes, I could still feel it – I was in another world. It was horrible, awful. I thought I was still in the dream. I tried to force myself awake. Then I opened my eyes and the world was gone – the dream was over. I was in my bedroom at home. I've never felt so relieved to wake up in my own bed!'

'Yeah,' I replied. 'I know that feeling.'

'But then I found this.' She held the pebble out to me again. 'I mean, I live by the beach. It's easy enough to find random pebbles around the place.'

'But you knew this wasn't a random pebble,' I said.

'I remembered the bit in the dream ...' She stopped.

'Where I gave it to you,' I said softly. 'One for you, one for Shona, as a mark of our friendship.'

Mandy bit harder on her lip. She didn't say anything, but she nodded. Then she seemed to make up her mind about something. She held the pebble out again. 'Here, take it,' she said. 'I mean, I know it's a mark of our friendship – but I don't need it. I know our friendship is strong – especially now. I don't want this. It scares me.'

I took the pebble and put it in my pocket. 'I've been there,' I whispered. 'I know exactly what you're going through.'

Mandy spoke in a whisper. 'You really were there with me? You saw the future too?' she asked. She sounded like a frightened child. 'It wasn't a dream at all – it was real. That's *it*? That's what we've got to look forward to? That's what my life is going to become?'

'Well, that's *one* version,' I replied.

'One version?'

'I guess you don't remember the last time we had this conversation?' I asked.

'Huh? What d'you mean? We've never had this conversation before.'

'Not this one, maybe. But one like it. Where I told you about the future and you didn't believe me.'

'Emily, I don't understand. You're not making sense. What are you—?'

'It's happened to me twice,' I said. 'I've seen two futures – and they were both as horrific as each other.'

'Two futures,' Mandy said numbly.

For a moment, I didn't know where or how to start. Then I decided to do it with actions instead of words.

I opened my jacket pocket and pulled out the

wishing stone. I held it out to show Mandy. 'Remember this?'

'The stone you had in the future too.'

'That's right. But I didn't tell you everything about it.'

'Go on.'

For a moment, I hesitated. Would she laugh at me? Then I looked at her face. I couldn't imagine her laughing at anything right now. 'It's — it's got powers,' I said. 'Magical powers. But scary too. It's kind of unpredictable.'

Mandy's frown deepened. 'Emily, you're not making any sense,' she said.

I put the stone back in my pocket and started again. 'OK,' I said. 'I'll explain everything.'

And this time, as I told Mandy all about the stone and the wishes and the underwater river and the two horrible futures, two things happened that hadn't happened before: she listened to every word and she believed me.

When I'd finished, Mandy's face was as white as the lines around the wishing stone. 'So now what?' she asked. 'You have one more wish, yes?'

'Yep.'

'So one more chance to make things turn out right. Make *everything* turn out right?'

'I guess. I just don't know how to ask the right question, how to phrase the wish so it doesn't twist it into something horrible for *someone*.'

'Yeah. I see what you mean.'

We fell silent for a moment. Then I remembered the PSHE lesson. 'But there's something else,' I said.

'What's that?'

I opened my other pocket. 'This.' Holding out the elephant, I said, 'I think it's telling me something.'

Mandy examined the elephant. 'What's it telling you?'

'The parable Mr Goode just shared with us,' I went on, 'about the men only seeing one bit of the elephant and thinking that was the whole story. Well, that's kind of what happened in each future. Each one worked out amazingly for one side – and terribly for the other.'

'And you reckon that's what *this* elephant is telling *us*?' Mandy finished.

'Exactly. We have to find a way to make things work out for *both* sides.'

'OK,' Mandy agreed. 'So how do we do that?'

'Good question,' I said, suddenly feeling hopeless. 'I haven't got a clue.'

The first lesson after lunch was art. I vaguely remembered being here before – but it felt as though that had been a dream. The first time, I'd been too miserable to care about what was happening around me. The second time, I'd been in too much shock to even notice. This time Mandy and I sat together, silent and separate from the rest of the class. We'd talked all the way through lunch break and still hadn't come up with an idea for my third wish.

Nor had we come up with a way to use the elephant parable to stop everything from going horrendously wrong. Until Ms Macmillan folded her arms, smiled at the class and started to speak.

'Welcome back to school,' she said brightly. Ms Macmillan generally said everything brightly. It was just the kind of teacher she was. 'This is my favourite term,' she said. Then she paused a beat before adding, 'Well, this one and the spring term and the summer term. It's my *joint* favourite.'

Most of the class laughed. Mandy and I continued to stare ahead of us. We must have looked like zombies.

'But this one is special,' Ms Macmillan went on. 'Because it's a *beginning*. And there is something so hopeful and positive about the start of something – especially the start of a new year. Don't you agree?' She paused for a millisecond before continuing. 'The start of a new year is a time when we make new promises, try new things. It's a time when I think that anything is possible. And just this morning, I received a letter that fits *perfectly* with my mood.'

She fumbled on her desk, then picked up a piece of paper and unfolded it. She cleared her throat and read from the piece of paper.

'We are launching a nationwide competition for all schoolchildren in Years Seven and Eight. The theme: Make a Piece of Art to Change the World!'

Ms Macmillan beamed as she looked around the class. Thirty blank faces looked back at her.

'Does that sound too much for you?' Ms Macmillan asked, a tiny note of uncertainty creeping into her voice.

Julie Crossens put her hand up. I felt a bit bad as she was sitting with a couple of other girls and I knew she'd probably rather be with Mandy. Right now, though, Mandy needed me more.

'Yes Julie?'

'Miss, how can art change the world?' Julie asked.

Ms Macmillan clapped her hands together as though Julie had just told her the school had won the lottery. 'Wonderful question!' she said. 'And that is *exactly* the point of this competition: how *can* art change the world? In exploring the question, I hope you will not only make some wonderful art, but find some interesting answers too.' She gave the class one last look. 'We will work together as a class. You can have whatever resources we have in the art department, and if you need any more then I'll do whatever I can to help you find them. And of course, you'll need your imaginations. To begin with, let's join up in pairs and brainstorm some ideas. Any questions?'

No one spoke. Ms Macmillan grinned. 'Great. Let's go. Find a partner and work in pairs. Let's see what ideas you come up with.'

Mandy chewed the end of her pencil. We'd agreed to work together. I couldn't help a tiny bit of me thinking that, if nothing else, at least Mandy and I were friends again. It was one thing to be grateful for. Even if it currently felt a bit like two hopeless people hanging on to each other as they traipsed blindly through a dark scary night.

'This is a good thing,' I said.

Mandy raised an eyebrow. 'Which bit of it is a good thing?' she asked miserably.

'This project. The fact that we have to come up with a way to change the world.'

Mandy raised her other eyebrow. 'And that's a good thing how, exactly?'

'Because that's exactly what we *need* to do. It's what we *want* to do. Look, I made a wish – twice

– to try to make things better. Both times, the wishing stone messed it up really badly.'

'OK ...'

'It messed the *world* up really badly.'

'So you're saying ...'

'I'm saying we have a chance to come up with an idea to change the world. *Stop* it from getting messed up. In school time!'

'OK, yeah. It's a good thing,' Mandy agreed. 'So what's your idea?'

'That's the only problem,' I admitted. 'I haven't thought of one yet.'

Then Mandy said the thing I'd been trying to avoid saying. Trying to avoid even thinking.

'What about the wishing stone?' she asked in a whisper. 'You've got one more wish. Could you use it to help us come up with something?'

The thought turned my stomach to ice. Could I? I mean, it would be so easy to take the stone out of my pocket, right now, and wish for it to help us come up with an amazing idea to change the world. Maybe we'd win the competition at the same time!

But what if its 'dark frame' took over again? What if it changed the world – but for the worse? What if it found a way of granting my wish that made things go wrong for *everyone*?

'I really don't know,' I said to Mandy. 'Maybe as a last resort, but let's see if we can think of anything else first.'

Mandy looked relieved. 'I agree,' she said.

I turned the elephant over and over in my hand as I thought. I liked the feel of it; it was comforting. I glanced around the class as I did it, watching everyone in their pairs, talking, scratching their heads, frowning.

'Another minute and then we'll share our ideas,' Ms Macmillan suddenly announced.

'Wait. That's it!' I said to Mandy.

'That's what?'

'Sharing our ideas. That's what we need to do!'

'Ye-e-e-s. That's what Ms Macmillan has *told* us we're doing,' Mandy said.

'Not just us,' I went on. 'Not just our class, or our year, or even our school. We need to bring *everyone* together. We need to get Shiprock and Brightport to work *together.*'

I held the elephant out to Mandy. 'Think about the elephant story. Each man only knew about one part of the elephant, so he only believed one part of the truth. That's what keeps happening with these futures.'

'If you only focus on one part of it, you can never fix the whole of it,' Mandy murmured, finally getting where I was coming from.

I grinned. 'Exactly! And we need to put all the truths together. Yours, mine, Shona's, Shiprock's Brightport's – everyone's!'

Mandy laughed. 'No pressure, then.'

I laughed back. 'OK, maybe not every single person. But the kids. Maybe we could work with Shona's class at Shiprock – come up with something together.'

As I said the words, I realised how much I needed us to do it. Not just to change the world or win a competition. Not even just to bring Shiprock and Brightport together. Yes, those things would be fantastic if we could achieve them. But at the centre of my idea was something that had been at the heart of both wishes I'd made: Shona, Mandy and I working together to create something beautiful. Whether or not it would change the world, I had no idea. What I did know was that it was the best way to fix the thing that I'd tried to mend with both of the wishes I'd made and the stone had ruined: our friendship.

'We make a piece of art together?' Mandy asked. 'That's what you're saying?'

'Yeah,' I said nervously. 'What d'you think?'

Mandy smiled. 'I think it's brilliant. We work with Shiprock to show what we can achieve together! *That's* how we'll change the world.'

'Yeah,' I agreed. 'And there's something else, too.'

'You mean that isn't enough?'

I shook my head. I'd had another thought. 'We have to make the piece of art by Friday.'

'Friday? But Ms Macmillan said we've got a week.'

'But it's not just about the competition,' I said. 'We're doing it to stop things from going wrong.' I paused before continuing. 'Each time I've made a wish, part of why it's gone wrong has come back to the same thing, the same people.'

'Midas,' Mandy said.

'Yup. Their meeting is on Friday. We need to exhibit our piece of art at the same time as the meeting.'

'And make it so amazing that everyone will come and see us, and no one will turn up to the meeting.'

'Right. Then Midas won't invest in the town,' I said.

'And they won't get to destroy Brightport *or* Shiprock.'

'Exactly.'

Mandy looked deflated. 'In other words, achieve the impossible,' she said.

I grinned at her. 'Not impossible at all,' I said. 'Especially when we already have you, me and Shona on the case.'

'Shona? But she's not even here.'

'No,' I agreed. 'But she was in the future, too. She fell asleep with the friendship pebble in her hand, just like you did. Which means that hopefully she has come back from that time to the present as well.'

'And she'll know how bad things will get if we don't do something about it,' Mandy added.

'Correct.' I smiled. 'So, are you in?'

At last, Mandy smiled back. 'You bet I'm in,' she said.

I smiled back at my friend. 'Great. Let's do it.'

And before I could talk myself out of it or wonder if I was doing the right thing, I'd put my hand in the air.

Ms Macmillan nodded at me. 'Yes, Emily?'

I stood up and cleared my throat. 'Miss, this piece of art,' I began. I hesitated before going on. 'If we want to change the world, we'd stand a better chance of doing it if we *all* worked together.'

'We will be doing,' Ms Macmillan replied. 'We're going to come together in a moment and share our ideas as a group.'

'No,' I pushed on. 'I don't mean just our class.' My heart banged as, in a flash, I saw it all go past my eyes: my fears of being found out as a mermaid at the start of Year Seven; the gulf between the two communities; my desperate desire to fit back into life at Brightport High. And then I remembered something else – the way I'd felt at the end of my adventure on a pirate ship.

I thought I didn't care what others thought of me, and that their opinions couldn't hurt me. But I'd realised that that wasn't strictly true. I *did* care. I cared a lot. I cared what my friends thought. I cared how I treated them and how they treated me. I cared about Brightport, Shiprock – I cared about the whole planet! Being independent and strong

218

didn't mean not caring. It meant figuring out which things really mattered and which things didn't. And I was in no doubt about what mattered right now.

'I think we should work with Shiprock School,' I said.

'Shiprock School?' Ms Macmillan asked.

'It's a—'

'It's a school for merfolk.' Mandy had pushed her chair back and was standing up next to me. 'Emily's idea is that we work together, the two schools. And I agree.'

'We could talk to Shona,' I said. 'I'm sure she'd get her class involved.'

'Who's Shona?' Ms Macmillan asked.

Before I had time to say anything, Mandy had replied. 'She's one of our best friends.'

My heart swelled so much in my chest it felt as if it were going to burst out of me. I swallowed down the emotion and somehow managed to squeak, 'If we really want to change the world, we should really do it together.'

There was a moment's pause.

Then Julie Crossens stood up. 'I agree,' she said. 'I think it sounds like a brilliant idea.'

I turned and gave Julie a grateful smile. She grinned broadly back at me.

'I think it sounds like a great plan.' I turned to see who'd spoken. It was Sherry Daniels. She'd stood up too.

Next up was Tammy Bayfield. 'I'm in,' she said.

One by one, everyone in the class stood up and declared their support for the idea.

Well, almost everyone. Aiden Harris was the only one still sitting down. Was he going to spoil it? Had we come this far only to let one person ruin it?

A moment later, he answered my unspoken questions. Kicking back his seat, he shrugged, then stood up and raised his fist in the air. 'I'm in,' he said. 'Let's change the world!'

Ms Macmillan let a slow smile creep across her face. '8P,' she said. 'I could not be prouder. Come on, then. Get your thinking caps on, and let's see what ideas we can come up with before we get Shiprock on board.'

As everyone gathered around, throwing out ideas, putting hands up, interrupting each other, talking over each other, laughing, teasing and scribbling ideas down, I felt something stir inside me for the first time in days.

Hope.

CHAPTER 18

It was later that day and I was on my way to Shiprock to see Shona.

My mind was still racing from the day's events. Everyone had come out of art on a high. We had a plan. A brilliant plan. An exciting plan.

I just needed two things. I needed Shona to have seen the future too, so she knew how bad it was going to get, and how important this was. And I needed her to persuade Shiprock to join up with us and put on an art display by the end of the week – which, if I thought about it, was a pretty big ask.

So I decided not to think about it. I forced my mind to go blank as I swam around the big rocks at the outer part of the town and across the wide space in the centre. Two grown-up mermaids swam by, chatting to each other as they passed me. Just like the last time I did this. It felt like a lifetime ago.

I smiled at the merbaby in the sling as they passed me. I smiled at the older merman with the long beard. Then I reached the opening that led to the caves on the west side of Shiprock, where Shona lived.

Shona's mum was swimming out of the entrance, like last time.

'Hey Emily, I'm just going out,' she said. 'Shona's in her room. Go on in. She'd love to see you.'

'Thanks, Mrs Silkfin,' I replied.

I swam inside, waiting for Shona to swim out to meet me like last time, and tell me excitedly about her day.

But Shona didn't swim out.

'Shona?' I called, as I swam through the caves of their home. I found her in her bedroom.

She barely looked up as I swam towards her. She was perched on a rock in front of her mirror, staring at her face.

'Hey,' I said.

Shona looked at me in the mirror. 'Hi, Emily,' she said. Then she looked back at herself in the glass. 'That's me in there, right?' she asked. 'I mean, like, me: Shona, mermaid, thirteen years old. That's who you see, right?'

I knew immediately what was going on.

'That's who I see,' I said.

Shona nodded, but still wouldn't look away.

I reached out to touch her arm. 'You can talk to me,' I said.

Shona didn't reply. She just kept staring at herself, as though she couldn't believe what she was seeing.

'I know what you're feeling,' I said.

Shona laughed, a bitter sharp laugh. 'I doubt it,' she said.

As I looked at her, I noticed something on a rock beside the mirror: the friendship pebble. I picked it up and held it out to her.

'I gave you this,' I said. 'I was there. So was Mandy. I *know* what you are going through.'

Shona's face turned white as she looked at the pebble. 'I don't want it,' she said in a shaky voice. 'I'm sorry – I know it's special, but it's freaking me out even being near it.'

'OK,' I said, putting it in my pocket with Mandy's. 'I'll hold on to it for now and give it back to you when you feel better about things.'

'It really happened?' she whispered. 'We were really there together?'

I nodded.

Shona's eyes went glassy and wide. 'I don't know how to deal with it,' she said as a big tear rolled out of each eye, trickled down her cheeks and melted away into the seawater.

I smiled at my best friend. 'Well, luckily I do,' I told her. 'Come on, let's get out of here. Let's go to our place and talk.'

Shona nodded, slipped off her perch and followed me out of her room. We swam silently to Rainbow Rocks.

'You don't remember the other time we were here, do you?' I asked as we swam up to the rocks.

Shona looked confused. 'Last night? When you gave me the friendship pebble? I thought—'

'No. Not last night. The other version of today,' I said nervously.

'The *other* version of today?'

'No, I didn't think so. Mandy didn't remember it either,' I said. 'But we've been here before. You told me about your school project.'

Shona's tail flicked against the rock. 'You know about the school project?' she asked.

I nodded. 'The one about plastics.'

Shona lifted a shoulder in a slow shrug. 'Not that it matters anyway,' she said. 'I've seen how things turn out.'

'It *does* matter,' I insisted. 'It matters more than ever!'

'Why, when there's nothing we can do about it?' Shona asked. Before I could reply, she went on. 'Sure, it won't be too bad for us in Shiprock, but for you and for Mandy and for everyone in Brightport . . . I can't bear to think of the world we're all going to end up in. Especially you guys. Everything's going to turn out horrible and mean and unfair, and we just have to sit back and watch it happen.'

'But that's what I'm trying to tell you. We *don't* have to sit back and watch it happen. We can do something about it. We *are* doing something about it.'

'Who's "we"?' Shona asked.

'Brightport High. Year Eight. And . . . um . . . you.'

Shona pointed at herself. 'Me?'

'Yeah. There's a competition. We have to come up with a way to change the world through art. And we have to put on the display this Friday.'

Shona snorted. 'Seriously?'

'Seriously. And we want to make it a combined thing with Shiprock.'

Shona pulled a face. 'I can't see that happening. We're working on our project all week,' she said. 'We won't have time to do anything else.'

'Shona,' I said. 'What is your project?'

'We've got to come up with some brilliant ingenious way of improving the—' Shona stopped. 'Oh,' she said.

I grinned at her. 'See?'

Shona let a hint of a smile sneak on to her face. 'We want the same thing,' she said.

'We do.'

'So we could work together.'

'We can.'

Shona's face finally broke into a broad grin. 'What are we waiting for, then?' she asked. 'Let's get planning!'

I threw my arms around her and hugged her as tightly as I could without completely squashing her.

'What's that for?' Shona asked, laughing as I pulled away.

'I'm happy,' I said. 'We're going to save the world.'

And we're going to save our friendship, I thought. Which was just as good, as far as I was concerned.

The days passed in a haze of activity.

First job was to bring the two classes together. We arranged to meet up on the beach on Tuesday after school.

Ms Macmillan came down to the beach with us, and we watched as Shona's class swam into the bay.

Mandy and Shona and I introduced everyone while Ms Macmillan and Mr Finsplash talked at the water's edge. Most of the kids pulled off their socks and shoes and waded out so we could get together with the Shiprock folk. To be fair, half of them ran straight out again as the water was freezing – but seeing them even make the effort was enough to warm my heart.

Between the two classes we agreed on a plan. The first step was to collect abandoned bottles, cans, plastic bags from the beaches and from the sea.

Alana, one of the mermaids in Shona's class, splashed her tail on the water. 'There's an empty cave near us in Shiprock,' she said. 'We could use that for storing anything we find in the sea.'

'That's brilliant,' I said. 'Thanks, Alana.'

'And anything we find on the beaches we could store at my parents' amusement arcade,' Mandy suggested. 'It's nearby and open every day.'

Alana smiled at Mandy. 'We'll be the two points of contact for collections then,' she said.

Mandy tried to look her usual tough self, but I could see she felt pleased to have such an important role.

'What do we do after we've collected enough stuff?' one of the merboys in Shona's class asked.

'Good question, Drake,' one of the others said. 'We need some way of bringing things together.'

We thought for a moment. Then Sherry jumped up so suddenly she nearly slipped on an incoming wave. 'My dad's a fisherman!' she said. 'Maybe he and some of the other fishermen could collect everything in their boats.'

'That's a swishy idea!' Shona said.

'Let's collect any abandoned fishing nets we come across too,' another mermaid called Meriel said. 'We can use them to hold everything together.'

'I'll ask Dad if we can use some of his old nets too,' Sherry said.

Aiden kicked at the water with his feet. 'Maybe I could speak to my dad too,' he suggested. 'See if he can find anything at the tip.'

Aiden's words had set a thought alight inside my mind. A way of getting Aiden's dad to the beach. 'Maybe he could use one of his trucks to bring everything down to the beach?' I suggested.

Aiden shrugged. 'I'll ask him. I don't see why not.'

That was part one in place. Part two would be where things got *really* exciting.

'OK, so we're ready,' I said. 'Everyone knows what they're doing. Let's meet up again on Thursday to bring everything together, and we'll be ready to go live on Friday night,' I suggested. 'How does that sound?'

'We could meet at the end of the pier,' Mandy suggested. 'That's easy for both sides to get to.'

Tammy put her hand up. 'I've got an idea,' she said. 'It might be silly though.'

Alana was in the water beside her. 'Nothing's silly,' she said. 'We're all in this together and every idea is a good one, right?'

'Right,' everyone agreed.

'Well, I was thinking maybe I could ask my mum to put an article in *The Brightport Times*, telling everyone to come to the promenade on Friday evening. What d'you think?' Sherry asked.

The roar of applause from two whole classes of kids was loud enough to make both teachers jump.

'I reckon that's what we think,' I said.

'Tell your mum it's a once-in-a-lifetime "Living Art" display,' Drake said. 'Maybe she'll put it on the front page!'

Sherry smiled shyly at Drake. 'Good idea,' she said.

'So, we're all set,' I said. 'Everyone knows what they're doing. Let's go for it!'

We worked on it all week. We barely thought about anything else. Both sides did what we'd agreed; meeting up to plan, shape and create our piece of art. Every day, we swapped ideas, building on the plan bit by bit each day, working together – making sure we looked at it from every side.

Almost too soon, Friday arrived. We managed to persuade Mrs Porter and Ms Macmillan to let us spend the whole of Friday putting the final touches to it. Shona said her class were doing the same. By the end of the day, it had finally taken shape. We were ready.

Nearly. There was still something I had to check. I wandered to the other side of the art room.

'Hey, Aiden,' I said, keeping my voice as casual as I could.

Aiden glanced at me. 'What's up?' he asked.

'Is your dad still OK to use his truck later?'

'Yeah, he's fine with it. He asked one of his men to bring it,' Aiden replied casually.

'*One of his men?*' I burst out.

Aiden frowned. 'Yeah. Why?'

Because in the last version of this day, your dad spent Friday night meeting with Mr Whittaker and the rest of the Midas crooks and then they invested in his company and ended up destroying the town. And we can't let that happen again!

I couldn't exactly tell Aiden that.

'Um . . .' I began.

What could I tell him? My mind was racing. The plan was going to fall apart. What could I do? I still had an option I barely dared think about: the wishing stone. Could I use it to wish that the meeting would be cancelled or that Mr Whittaker went down with flu or—?

Aiden was still talking. 'He was meant to be going to some meeting, so he asked George if he'd do it,' he said. 'But now I think about it, Mum told him that this is more important. She told him to do it himself. So yeah, he'll be there.'

'Really?' I asked. I nearly hugged him. It was only Mandy excitedly grabbing hold of my sleeve that stopped me. 'Your dad is definitely going to be there?' I insisted.

'Yeah. Really,' Aiden said. 'Why? What's the problem?'

I laughed. 'No problem,' I said, turning to grin at Mandy as my heart finally came back down to its normal rate. 'No problem at all.'

It was half an hour before show time and everything was in place. Aiden's dad had been as good as his word and brought our artwork to the beach. We kept it covered as we waited at the water's edge so we didn't ruin the surprise. Tammy told us her mum was on her way down with a reporter and photographer. She had printed an announcement in yesterday's paper about the event and promised they would cover it today.

Sherry's dad was heading out to sea with his fishermen pals for the part we'd persuaded them to play.

I waited with Mandy and the rest of the class on the beach. It was starting to get dark so it was hard to tell, but I thought I saw some shapes on the horizon.

Julie was next to Mandy. She suddenly pointed out to sea. 'They're coming,' she said. 'I see them!'

'OK,' I replied. 'Action stations! Let's go!'

And with that, we picked up our creation, carrying it out to the water's edge and waiting for the Shiprock merfolk.

A couple of minutes later, Shona and a few of her classmates swam up.

'All set?' I asked, as they took it away from us.

'All set,' Shona replied.

'Good luck!' we called to them.

As we stood on the beach watching them swim away, Mandy nudged me. 'Look,' she said.

'I *am* looking,' I replied, without taking my eyes off the sea.

'No. Not out to sea. Over there.' She pointed behind us.

I turned to see what she was pointing at. People were walking along the promenade. I watched where they were heading.

Please don't be going to the Midas meeting. Please be coming to see us.

Everyone was turning to look. Soon, we all found ourselves watching, grinning, clapping our hands as, one after another, the groups, the couples, the individuals and families all made their way towards us.

All of them.

'Yes!' I whispered under my breath.

Soon there was quite a crowd on the beach. Couples walked hand in hand along the sand; little kids in woolly hats and gloves clung to their parents; mums and dads called to their children who were too busy running up and down the beach and looking out to sea to hear their parents.

Suddenly, Sherry's mobile phone beeped. She checked the screen. 'It's my dad,' she called to us. 'They're ready.'

I peered into the fading light of the sea and sky. I could vaguely make out the shapes, silhouetted against the darkness.

And then the lights came on.

The fishing boats were spread out in a semi-circle in the bay. At the exact same moment they all switched on their lights and lit up the shape in the centre of the bay: the plastic we'd spent all week collecting, tying together and shaping.

I watched as two mermaids swam to the edges where we'd joined everything together. They undid the ropes, and the structure burst open.

Hundreds and hundreds of bottles and tubs and cartons had been joined end to end, woven across each other, built into the giant structure that bounced into shape before our eyes. As the light from the fishing boats hit it, it was clear to see that it was a giant, plastic, multicoloured net.

Mermaids and merboys swam and danced and twirled in the waves. Their tails sparkled like rainbows as they jumped into the net, wriggling in the gaps, grasping at the plastic.

Half of the group swam right into the middle of the net while the other half swam around the edge. The merkids on the outside then grabbed the ends of the net to form a circle and trapped their classmates in it.

People on the beach gasped as they watched.

'Daddy, Daddy, the merboy got trapped in the plastic net!' I heard a little boy exclaim.

A little girl nearby pulled on her mum's sleeve. 'I want to help the mermaids!' she cried.

Her mum sighed as she watched the display. 'So do I, sweetheart,' she said. 'So do I.'

I felt a tear trickle down my cheek as I watched Shona's class playing their part in our living art. It was mesmerising. It was breathtaking. And it was powerful.

I couldn't stop myself from smiling through my happy tears.

We'd really done it. We'd made a piece of art to change the world.

CHAPTER 19

*T*he display had nearly finished. Most people were still watching open-mouthed when Aiden came over to me. 'My dad's gonna head off now,' he said. 'He says one of his guys will help us clear up afterwards.'

My smile froze. 'What? Why's he leaving?' I asked.

'He wants to get to that meeting,' Aiden said. 'Turns out he had time to do both. Great result all round, eh?'

'No!' I yelled. It wasn't a great result at *all*! It was a terrible, awful result!

'No?' Aiden echoed.

'He can't go,' I said. 'He can't leave. He mustn't go to that meeting!'

Aiden scowled at me. 'What are you talking about? Why does it bother *you* if my dad goes to a meeting?'

I grabbed Aiden's sleeve. 'Ask him to stay,' I urged. 'Just for five minutes. It's not finished.'

'It's *nearly* finished,' Aiden argued. 'I don't under—'

'Please, Aiden,' I insisted. 'I can't explain. Just trust me. Make him stay five more minutes.'

Aiden shrugged. 'OK, whatever. I'll try,' he said and he turned to catch up with his dad.

I had five minutes to think of a way to stop the future from going wrong. After all we'd done, everything we'd been through, I couldn't let it happen. I just couldn't.

I dug my hands in my pockets to warm them up. The wishing stone. My fingers closed around it.

Could I do it? *Should* I do it? I had one last wish. I could use it, right now. Make my wording so clear that there was no way it could turn things bad.

Did I dare, though? However I worded it, I had the feeling the stone was crafty enough that it would find some way to twist my words and make things go horribly wrong, one way or another. Could I afford to take the risk?

Could I afford *not* to?

My thoughts wrestled and twisted as the seconds ticked by. And then . . .

'Emily!'

Someone was calling me. I opened my eyes and peered around.

'Em! Look!' It was Mandy. She was pointing out to sea. In the darkness, I could see a swell building up. Waves were starting to crash heavily on the beach.

What was going on? Was it a sudden winter storm? The wake from a container ship out at sea? Or . . .?

Neptune.

His chariot glinted in the darkness as it rode through the waves towards us. And then we saw him, sitting high up on it, tail looped over the side, trident held aloft. A few of my classmates gasped as his chariot came to the shore.

I glanced behind me and saw Aiden talking animatedly to his parents. His dad shrugged and nodded.

Good. He hadn't left yet. Now I just had to keep him here as long as I could.

I ran down to the water's edge. 'Your Majesty,' I said, breathlessly.

Neptune's eyes found mine. They were glinting with anger. 'I believe someone around here has GOLD!' he boomed.

'What? No! There's no gold,' I said.

Neptune reached into his chariot and grabbed something. A crumpled piece of paper. He waved it at me. 'Well then, tell me, why did one of my loyal staff give me THIS? And who is this Midas fellow who claims he turns *everything* to gold?'

I stepped towards him, peering at the scrap of paper in his hand. As he waved it, I realised what it was. A crumpled, torn, soggy leaflet for the Midas meeting – only most of it had been ripped away. All Neptune had was the top half of it, the half with the headline that said: ***Does Your Business Need the MIDAS Touch? We turn everything we touch to GOLD.***

'Your Majesty, sir,' I began, 'it's a company, not a person, and they're not *actually* turning things into gold.'

'They're not?' Neptune asked. As he spoke, the swell dropped a little.

'No. It's a – what do you call it?'

'It's a metaphor.'

I turned to see who'd spoken. It was a woman I vaguely recognised. She stepped out from the crowds who were mostly staring in wonder at Neptune.

'Rachel Bayfield, editor of *The Brightport Times*,' she said as she held her hand out towards Neptune. 'I wonder if I might interview you for our newspaper?'

Neptune narrowed his eyes at her.

'It'll be on the front page,' Mrs Bayfield said. 'With a photo and everything.'

Neptune patted at his white hair. 'Well,' he said. 'I don't see why not. I will instruct my dolphins to clean up my chariot first.'

That was when I noticed them: the dolphins were underwater all around Neptune's chariot. Hidden in the darkness.

Something was prickling at the edge of my thoughts. What was it? Something to do with the dolphins.

Neptune was holding his trident out, leaning over to call to them when—

Yes! That was it!

'Wait!' I said.

Neptune turned to me, his eyebrows raised so high they made his hairline extra bushy. '*WAIT*?' he asked, in a voice that made me feel about the size of a sardine.

I gulped hard. 'There's something you have to do for us.'

'*HAVE* to do? For *YOU*?' he questioned.

'I mean, please, sir. Your Majesty.'

I glanced round. Aiden's dad was looking at his watch. People were starting to slip away.

'We have to change the world,' I said to Neptune. 'We have to change the *future*.'

Neptune returned my stare. I fully expected him to order me to stop talking riddles and nonsense. But he didn't. As he held my eyes, something changed. His face softened. It was as though he could see inside me, see what I'd been through, what had happened, what was to come. It was as if he read it all in my eyes.

For a split second, I wondered if he had been through it too. Had he somehow seen the future himself and knew as clearly as I did that we couldn't leave it to chance? I'd probably never know. It didn't matter anyway because a moment later Neptune nodded.

And then in a soft voice he said, 'Very well. What do you need me to do?'

So I told him my idea. And after the briefest of pauses, he nodded again and agreed to my request.

All that was left now was to wait, and hope more than I'd ever hoped for anything else that it would work.

The dolphins put on an awe-inspiring display.

They leaped in giant arcs over our plastic net artwork. They twirled in perfect formation around the edges of it. They zig-zagged between mermaids, they jumped high in the air, their tails sprinkling multicoloured arcs of water below them. The fishermen lit up their every move.

My class gasped throughout the whole thing. So did every other person on the beach.

Amongst them, Aiden's dad – who had never before seen a dolphin – stood on the beach, tears streaming down his face, watching every moment and clapping at every trick.

And the best thing?

Mandy was standing beside me. I linked her arm as we watched. Behind us, hardly anything was happening on the prom. Everyone was on the beach. Which was how I noticed the vehicle driving along the lonely promenade.

'Look,' I said to Mandy.

She turned to see Mr Whittaker in the Midas Enterprises van. I watched him too, driving out of town after a meeting that not a single person showed up to.

The next morning, I swam over to Shiprock to catch up with Shona. I still hadn't stopped smiling.

As I moved through the cool water, I thought about the other times I'd taken this journey in the last few days – and how they'd all worked out.

A tiny thought was nagging at the edges of my mind: the stone. I *still* had that final wish.

I flicked my tail to tread water. After a moment of thinking about it, I took the stone from my pocket and studied it. I could feel its heat in my palm. It was growing warmer as I held it.

I swam on, the stone in my hand as I thought. I could do it – make one last wish.

The stone grew warmer. I felt it urging me on. *Do it. Do it.*

A few words and I could be there. I could ask the stone to show me the future. I could see how things worked out, confirm that we really had fixed things.

The stone was taking me there. I could already feel the current begin to pull me towards the river in the sea.

I'd made up my mind.

I stopped swimming. I flicked my tail hard, to hold my position against the force that was growing stronger and stronger with every second. I opened my palm and looked at the wishing stone.

It was buzzing so brightly that it danced in my hand. Its heat was filling my whole body with warmth. Its strength was starting to drag me into the tide. Any second now and I wouldn't have any choice in the matter.

This was it.

I gripped the stone and spoke loudly and quickly.

'I wish that the chasm in the seabed will close up and *never* let anyone slip through it again!'

And then I threw the wishing stone towards the chasm as hard as I could.

I watched as it flew away from me. As I gazed after it, the tide took hold of it and spun it around and around.

Then the current exploded as if it had been set on fire. In the middle of it, the wishing stone was bright white, spinning and dancing and throwing a rainbow of colours all around as it swirled away from me.

Further and further. The stone grew smaller and smaller, the ball of light faded, the chasm receded. A tiny speck of light remained – and then, with a final 'pop', it closed up and disappeared.

The current had gone: nothing was pulling at me.

The light had gone: nothing was dazzling me.

The stone had gone: nothing was urging me to give in to temptation and see how the future would work out.

It was over.

The sea felt calm and gentle as I continued on to Shiprock. My thoughts felt just as peaceful. There was only one way I would find out what was going to happen in the future and that was by living my life, day by day. I didn't need wishes. I didn't need answers. Things would unfold in their own way and in their own time. We had done everything we could to make things work out – but all I could *really* know about was today.

Beyond that the future was anyone's guess.

And I'd get there. Eventually. One day at a time.

I sat on a bench on the pier, looking out at the sea and thinking over everything that had happened.

Shona had been as happy as we were. It turned out Shiprock town was going to receive an award from Neptune for what the merfolk had done. He said anything that protected his oceans would always get his backing, and that he had pledged to work with anyone who was working to make a better world for us all.

As I sat there, thinking about how everything had worked out, I pulled the elephant out of my pocket. I smiled and turned it over in my hands. 'Thank you,' I whispered.

'Hi there, Emily.'

I looked up to see Millie coming towards me with a couple of bags of shopping in her hands.

'Well, that was quite something last night, wasn't it?' she said as she put her bags on the ground and sat down next to me on the bench.

I laughed. 'It certainly was.'

Millie nudged me and pointed at the elephant in my hand. 'That's nice,' she said.

I looked at the elephant, then at Millie. Something wriggled and fizzed inside my stomach. 'Millie,' I said, my voice coming out of me almost as if it belonged to someone else.

'Yes, love,' she replied.

I reached into my pocket and pulled out the two friendship pebbles. 'Can I give you something?' I asked.

Millie laughed. 'Of course you can.'

The wriggling and fizzing in my stomach exploded as I held the pebbles out to her. In that moment, I didn't know if we would be here again, or if we'd been here before, or if the future came first or the present could change the past. I didn't have any answers, and the questions themselves made my head spin. But I knew one thing:

I knew what I had to do.

'Here,' I said, handing her the pebbles. 'Keep them.'

'Really?' Millie asked as she took the pebbles from me. 'What d'you want me to do with these?'

I swallowed hard so I could get the words past the rock jamming my throat up. 'Promise me you'll never sell them or get rid of them and you'll keep them till the day you give them back to me. You'll know when the time is right.'

Millie laughed. 'You're talking in riddles, young lady.'

'I know I'm not making any sense to you now – and when you give them back to me, I won't think *you're* making any sense either,' I went on. 'I – I can't explain, but there's too much at stake not to do this. Make me take them back, even if I say I've never seen them before. Promise me you'll do it.'

Millie put the stones into her bag. 'For you, missy, I will do anything, however potty it might sound.'

'Thank you!' I reached out to hug her. As I did, the elephant slipped from my lap.

Millie caught it and held it out to me.

Smiling at Millie, I closed her hand over the elephant. 'Keep the elephant with the pebbles,' I said. 'They belong together.'

'Really? You're sure?'

'Absolutely positive,' I replied.

Millie pulled a handkerchief out of her coat pocket, wrapped the elephant in it and then put it into her bag with the pebbles. 'Thank you, lovey,' she said. 'I'll add it to my collection. You never know when it might come in handy.'

I laughed as she kissed me and stood up.

'You're right,' I whispered, as Millie walked up the pier and I closed my eyes in the fading light of a warm winter's day. 'You never know.'

EPILOGUE

The Brightport Times – 22 February
KIDS' WORLD-CHANGING ART KICKS
OFF NATIONWIDE CAMPAIGN

The Chronicle and Times group today announced the start of a nationwide campaign to clean up our towns, our beaches and our seas.

The campaign follows the extraordinary work of two very talented classes of children who worked together on a piece of 'Living Art' that caught the imagination of their towns.

Their project was last week awarded first prize

in a national competition to make a piece of art to change the world.

Brightport School's art teacher, Ms Macmillan, told *The Brightport Times*: 'I couldn't be prouder of my class. They are not only creative, intelligent and hard-working, but, together with Shiprock School, they have shown the rest of us what can be achieved when people collaborate and communicate.'

Shiprock teacher Mr Finsplash agreed: 'This is the start of something very special. Watch out, world. Our kids are taking you by storm!'

The Chronicle and Times group are proud to share their message with the world. Our campaign launches next week, with the aim of halving the amount of waste that goes into our oceans – and into our landfills – in the next ten years.

One of the young organisers, Emily Windsnap, told us: 'We learned in one of our lessons that everything is linked, and that if we only fix one side of a problem, we haven't fixed it at all. We hope everyone will join our campaign and we are so proud to have started it. Thank you to everyone who has helped up to now. We're excited to see what the future brings.'

We at *The Chronicle and Times* have only one thing to add to that: if this is what our young generation have to offer, we think the future is looking very bright indeed.